Castle

of

Misadventure

Paul Kanner Mystery 2

by

J. D. Demetre

drawings by S. E. Brett

All royalties from the sale of this book will be donated to Barnardo's children's charity.

For Sara and Joseph with all my love

Character Portraits

The following key characters were introduced in the first *Paul Kanner Mystery*, *Clean-Out*. These portrayals provide background material for new readers of the series as well as refreshing and extending previous readers' knowledge of these individuals.

 **Paul Kanner** is a 14-year-old boy who is in Year 10 at Hollenbeck High School in Greenwich, South-East London. Paul has what used to be termed Asperger's Syndrome and experiences some difficulties in making sense of other people. He is highly intelligent and enjoys playing various board games, including chess, as well as video-games on his

PS console. When at home, he spends most of his time in his room with Bella, his devoted and affectionate Yorkshire terrier/poodle (yorkiepoo), who tolerates the stinks and noises emanating from Paul's makeshift science laboratory. Paul is particularly unhappy at school, where his classmates and teachers alike are intolerant of his apparent aloofness and lack of conformity. His main tormentor there is John Cameron, who routinely plays tricks on Paul and causes him both humiliation and pain. Paul's parents care for him but find him difficult to deal with, hence the atmosphere at home is often tense, causing Paul to retreat to the sanctuary of his room and his dog. His chance meeting with Detective Sergeant Joe Bertolli (see below) near a burglary site led to Paul serving as a principal witness in a complicated case of serial burglary. Paul's keen observational and intellectual skills impressed the sergeant and led to him contributing to solving the case (the subject of the first Paul Kanner Mystery,

Clean-Out).

Bella is the Kanners' two-year-old yorkiepoo (a combination of Yorkshire terrier and poodle). She is very affectionate towards Paul but can also be rather feisty and demanding of his attention. She seems to be very good at gauging Paul's moods and is a great comfort to him, especially when he has had a particularly stressful day at school.

Detective Sergeant Joe Bertolli works for the Metropolitan Police at Greenwich Police Station. After a glittering start at Hendon Police

Academy, Joe has become increasingly disgruntled as his police career has failed to progress. His divorce five years ago contributed to this decline, though little is known about his former wife or the circumstances that led to the break-up. Highly intelligent and capable, the unkempt and eccentric 38-year-old's antics have left him almost friendless at work. Despite helping to solve some notable serious crime cases, his colleagues generally view him as lacking in the "right stuff" of a good police officer: being a good time-keeper; following orders; thinking in a straightforward police sort of way; and being a team-player. In the police station, he tries to go as unnoticed as his six-feet-four-inches of height allows him to be. His boss, DCI Sara Gravesham, despises him, though she occasionally expresses her grudging admiration for his ability to look at a case from a new angle. Since meeting Paul Kanner some months ago, he has felt a strong connection to this boy. His only friends at work are Dr Benjamin Zeigarnik and DC Maxine Carter (see portraits below).

Dr Benjamin Zeigarnik

is a forensic psychologist who works at the University of London as well as for the Metropolitan Police. The 57-year-old Russian studied Psychology at Moscow State University. Following a brief spell in an elite special forces unit (Spetsnaz) of the Soviet Army, he moved to London thirty years ago to continue his studies and work. During his early days in London, he had been befriended by the Historian Dr Luigi Pecorino (see below). He is the grandson of the famous Soviet psychologist, Dr Bluma Zeigarnik. He uses his large physical presence and flowing beard to advertise his colourful personality and to browbeat anyone who annoys him, whether they be a student, a university head of department or a senior police official. His highly analytical mind and waspish wit have won him many friends as well as some enemies. His favourite past-time is to jump on his metallic red Lambretta scooter and ride around the streets of central London, laughing at irate car-drivers stuck in traffic. He often dines at *Café Roma*, an Italian restaurant run by Luigi Pecorino. He first met Sgt Joe Bertolli during an assignment with the Metropolitan Police and their friendship grew quickly. He met Paul Kanner on Joe Bertolli's previous case (see *Clean-Out*) and was impressed with Paul's abilities and interests, which he likes to nurture.

Detective Constable Maxine Carter works for the Metropolitan Police at Greenwich Station and is a colleague and friend of Joe Bertolli. Before becoming a police officer, Maxine had been a maths whizz who had graduated from University College London only a few years ago. As much as she loved numbers, Maxine decided that she needed a life of action and applied to Hendon Police Academy the year after she'd left university. At Hendon, she was the top cadet, excelling in all the academic and physical disciplines on the curriculum. Maxine is now the station's main number-cruncher and computer geek, who on most days spends hours looking for meaningful patterns in various crime data sets. Colleagues at Greenwich Police Station perceive Maxine Carter as only slightly more normal than Joe

Bertolli. Her friendship with Joe is based on their mutual respect and shared feelings of being outsiders in the police force.

 **Dr Luigi Pecorino (also known as Chef Luigi) is** the owner of *Café Roma*, an Italian restaurant in Bloomsbury, Central London. Luigi grew up in Italy and studied history at the ancient University of Bologna. He moved to London fifty years ago, to continue his studies and eventually became a renowned historian at University College London. He was the first historian to discover that the Romans believed that different kinds of foods had an impact on mood and thinking. His book on the subject, *Roman Foodlore*, was highly regarded for being both entertaining and informative and won him several awards. Having a lively and

inquiring mind, Luigi combined his academic career with being an exquisite chef and a businessman. He only fully retired from university life two years ago at the age of 72. Dr Benjamin Zeigarnik first met Luigi thirty years ago at a public event at the university, and since that time, considered Luigi to be his substitute father and mentor. The two men frequently meet at Luigi's restaurant, where they often share jokes, stories and work-related problems. At times, they can be very competitive with each other when it comes to offering advice, as they both consider themselves to be very wise. Benjamin often discusses his police work with Luigi over a meal at *Café Roma*, where he has taken Paul Kanner and Sgt Joe Bertolli.

Chapter 1

A Day at the Castle

Lisa Khan lay on the ground of the inner bailey of the castle, barely registering the battlements that loomed twenty feet above her supine body. She could hear screams and disembodied voices but could not summon the energy to move her eyes or her head. Just a few seconds ago, she had been walking along the secured rampart to get a view of the rolling hills. She remembered positioning herself by a *crenel* between two *merlons* that were in the middle of the battlement wall. At least she could still remember these fancy words that Mr Snow had taught them in Tuesday's History class. Crenels, he'd explained, were gaps between the merlons that formed the castle battlement...it looked like a set of teeth (merlons) with every other tooth missing (crenels). Think of molars and cavities he said, extending his analogy to an absurd degree.

Mr Paul Snow, head of History at Hollenbeck High School in Greenwich hovered over the body of the fourteen-year-old student in a state of shock. He was surrounded by staff and students who instinctively kept their distance, waiting for the decisive moment...the one that never came. Mr Snow swooned and keeled over. He was struggling to catch his breath. His two teaching colleagues rushed to his aid as a number of students cried and screamed in abject terror. While uniformed castle staff attended to Lisa Khan, the two teachers worked to get Paul Snow on his back in order to keep his airways clear. Within minutes, the wail of a siren aroused the assembled group from their stupor. The paramedics' professional calm and soothing words helped to restore some sense of order. One of the paramedics leaned over to a teacher and gently delivered his preliminary diagnosis: the girl had a suspected broken back and the teacher probably had

had a heart-attack.

As the ambulance pulled away with the two hapless victims, the two remaining teachers, Ms Krista Mehl and Mr Terry Chadwick tried to corral and console the Year 10 students. Ms Mehl sprang into action, took out her mobile 'phone and called the coach-driver, suggesting that they should cut short their ill-fated visit to Jericho Castle. The students would be provided with drinks and sandwiches on the coach. Mr Chadwick would complete an incident-report form as soon as he returned to school. He reflected on the staff meeting that took place in the middle of last term. The most fiercely debated item on the agenda that day had been the trip to Jericho Castle that John Snow and he had proposed, arguing that visiting such an intact castle would provide a unique opportunity for students to learn about the architecture of English medieval castles. Several of their colleagues at the meeting had opposed the proposal, pointing out that the castle had been the scene of an unusually high number of mishaps. The newspapers and news-sites had been awash with headlines, some of which he had kept in his School History Trips file, such as...

The Curse of Jericho Castle

Jericho Claims another Victim

Jericho Jinx

Calamity Castle

As Mr Terry Chadwick was lost in his recollections of how he and John Snow had won the argument that had secured the visit, the other teacher, Ms Krista Mehl was musing on the impact of today's events on the students. Her thoughts turned to the students she considered to be the most sensitive and least robust and as she did so, her gaze naturally wandered in the direction of Paul Kanner. Paul had been very quiet throughout the visit, which was not at all unusual as he almost always kept himself to himself. Ms Mehl had noticed when they had all boarded the coach for the return journey that Paul had appeared even more distracted than usual and had been fiddling with his hair...a sign that he was very agitated by something or other. She looked at him now...seated on his own at the front of the coach, just two seats behind the driver. He seemed to be tracing outlines with an imaginary pencil on the back-rest of the seat in front of him.

Ms Mehl struggled to keep her balance as she forced herself up from her seat. Her ungainly journey towards Paul Kanner had ended with her being catapulted to the front of the coach as the driver very suddenly slowed down. Regaining her balance and her composure, she plonked herself next to Paul and manufactured her best smile. Of all the teachers at Hollenbeck School, she had probably been the most tolerant of Paul's aloof and uncooperative ways, and felt a mixture of sympathy and frustration in many of her dealings with him. With all that had happened on today's disastrous trip, she felt she had to show her most sympathetic side.

"Hello Paul. How are you?" Paul Kanner turned his head in Ms Mehl's direction but looked beyond her face as if looking through the far-side window. Paul's lips were taut and his eyebrows frowned in a picture of deep and unresolved concentration.

"Er...I was thinking about Lisa falling from the battlements. I can't understand how it happened."

"I know what you mean Paul. There's a solid safety rail running along the length of the rampart and a steel-mesh fence beneath this. I don't understand how she could have fallen into the bailey." Paul grunted lightly and returned his gaze back to the imaginary drawing on the back-rest of the seat in front of him.

Chapter 2

Old News

After an emotional reunion with his parents, which became fraught with their anxieties, Paul Kanner retreated to his bedroom to be with his own thoughts. Before he had time to close his bedroom door, Bella, his yorkiepoo dog bounded through the gap and gave him a yappy greeting. Bella was one of the few beings that consistently raised his spirits and made him smile. He lifted Bella so that she could give him a face-lick and then settled at his small desk by the window, with Bella in attendance on the floor next to his chair.

Paul had not known Lisa Khan particularly well, but was very upset by the accident she had endured at Jericho Castle. Paul was particularly affected by the apparent incomprehensibility of the event. As Ms Mehl had said, it was difficult explaining Lisa's fall from the rampart when it was secured by a sturdy rail of steel tubing and a steel mesh fence. He estimated that the rail was about five feet off the base of the rampart...Lisa would have had to collide into the railing with considerable force for her to have fallen over it...like running into it at speed. As the rampart was only about eight feet wide, there was no way that Lisa could have picked up any real speed across such a short distance.

Googling "Jericho Castle" gave Paul 135 hits. He was hoping to find a detailed drawing of the castle to help him visualise how Lisa Khan could possibly have fallen from the battlement rampart to the bailey. The latest entries in the results list concerned new safety features introduced at the castle to counteract the negative publicity surrounding the spate of unfortunate incidents that had occurred. The most frequent entries related to the various accidents that had occurred at Jericho Castle between 2015 and last year. The oldest entries seemed to focus on the history of the castle and its key architectural features, including an article in *The History Teacher* journal. Paul gazed at the results list in horror. He was surprised that there was so much coverage of accidents. *Weren't the teachers at Hollenbeck aware of all this news?*

Opening and scanning the various sites helped Paul establish that there had been thirty-one serious incidents at the castle over a period of five years. Lisa's accident was presumably number 32. After analysing the 31 incidents in as much detail as he could glean from the variable quality of the news reports, Paul tabulated the findings, to help him make sense of it all.

Paul was overwhelmed by the number and seriousness of the incidents that had occurred. He had tabulated the numbers to impose a sense of order on the unexpected flurry of reports he'd read, but his mind was reeling and flitting from one question to another. *How come this place is still open to the public?* Most of the visitors seemed to be kids on school visits, as reflected in the fact that about two-thirds of the incidents involved kids between the ages of 8 and 16.

Didn't schools know about the terrible safety record of the place? Why hadn't the local council or the police closed the place down? From what he could tell from the reports, the police only became involved in two cases: a teacher dying from injuries caused by masonry falling from a wall-buttress; and a university historian who appeared to have gone missing when visiting the castle chapel. The number of 'explained' cases were themselves a cause for concern, suggesting that the structural maintenance of the place had been neglected. Even more puzzling was the high number of incidents that had been unexplained: twelve of the injury cases plus the missing historian. It was not crystal clear what 'unexplained' meant...*did it simply mean that the accidents were not caused by blatantly obvious structural faults, or could it be that...*

Before he could continue with his train of thought, Paul was abruptly forced into the present moment by Bella growling and tugging at the hem of his jeans.

Number of Incidents by Castle Location and Explanations in Media Reports				
Incident	**Location**		**Explanation**	
Broke bones in a fall (11 cases, *12 cases including Lisa*)	Ramparts *7 including Lisa*	6	Crumbling of surface	3
			Loose railing	1
			Unexplained	2
			3 unexplained including Lisa	
	Castle Keep	1	Slipped on step	1
	Watchtower	4	Loose step	2
			Unexplained	2
Head injury (18 cases)	Ramparts	8	Crumbling surface	3
			Loose railing	2
			Unexplained	3
	Castle Keep	3	Loose step	1
			Unexplained	2
	Barbican	7	Loose railing	2
			Loose step	2
			Unexplained	3
Death (1 case)	Chapel	1	Falling masonry	1
Gone missing (1 case)	Last seen in chapel	1	Unexplained	1

Chapter 3

Digging into the Past

Hollenbeck High School was abuzz with rumour, conspiracy theories and general pandemonium. Paul Kanner found it hard to believe that his class had returned from Jericho Castle only eighteen hours ago. He was going over the events of the previous day in his mind, thinking about how comfortable he'd felt within the confines of the castle. Unlike the other kids, his natural caution prevented him from exploring the higher reaches of the watchtowers and the keep, but he'd felt transported back in time nonetheless. He felt more secure there, walking about the bailey and exploring the dungeons than he'd ever felt at this school. It was such a pity that Lisa Khan's misadventures and Mr Snow's ill-health had cut short the visit to the castle. The word in school assembly was that Lisa would be in hospital for quite some time and would likely be paraplegic, wheelchair-bound for the rest of her life. Mr Snow was also still in hospital but was recovering well.

The morning's lessons seemed to fly by, though Paul had paid virtually no attention to the teachers. Instead, he continued his several trains of thought concerning Jericho Castle. Among other things, he had decided it would be a good idea to send an e-mail to his acquaintance, Sgt Joe Bertolli of the Metropolitan Police. Paul had been a witness in one of the sergeant's earlier cases and even contributed to the solution of the crime. Joe Bertolli had told Paul to stay in touch. Paul's concerns about Jericho Castle seemed an appropriate reason to contact the policeman. Paul decided to spend his lunch-break in the IT room so that he could write his e-mail and conduct some research in peace. He reached out for the double swing-doors leading to the Science Block corridor when he felt a slimy substance crawl down his hair. He couldn't resist the inquisitive urge to touch his head and when he brought his hand back in view it was covered in greeny-yellow glutinous gunge. He turned clockwise a full 360 degrees in an effort to discover the offending idiot who had thrown this at him. There were no obvious suspects in view. Attempting again to open the swing doors, Paul was assailed by a cacophony of hoots, demonic laughs and taunts...he might have guessed! The grinning face of John Cameron peered at him from round the corner.

"Did you miss me fool?"

Paul wished he had a magic wand to make this idiotic thug disappear. Before he could decide how to respond, three of Cameron's goons appeared at Cameron's side and renewed their taunts. Paul knew that John Cameron was much more likely to produce a violent display when in the presence of his goading cronies. He really didn't feel like being kicked and punched today. He remembered a conversation he'd had with the police psychologist Dr Benjamin Zeigarnik, a friend of Sgt Joe Bertolli, about being in tight corners...he had said do something that is unexpected to diffuse a potentially violent situation. So Paul did just that.

"Erm...John. Could you please do me a favour? I need your advice about something." John Cameron's face assumed an even more hostile expression and Paul began to think that he'd made a grave mistake in his adoption of this tactic.

"Well my aspie friend, what can I advise you about? Do you want me to explain how to be normal? Or maybe, how to look up to your superiors? Or maybe even how to dress so that you pass for a 21st century human?" Cameron and his cronies renewed their laughter at Paul's obvious bewilderment.

Paul tried again to forestall any violence. Calming his own fears and wearing his most endearing and earnest facial expression, he forced himself to look Cameron in the eye. "Seriously John, I do need your advice about something important. Can we talk alone for a second?"

John Cameron glanced at Paul, then looked at his three cronies. With an enigmatic smile, he shrugged his shoulders and walked over to Paul, who was surprised by the apparent success of his bargaining manoeuvre.

"What is it then Kanner? Don't waste my break-time."

"I need to talk to you in private" Paul replied.

Paul Kanner and John Cameron walked away from the other kids and headed towards the far end of the playground area. They walked together in a way that would have suggested to a naive observer that they were friends, not long-term bully and victim.

"Well Kanner, what is it? I haven't got all day!"

"I want to learn to play football properly so

that I could join in with the others. You're brilliant at the game, so I wondered whether you could teach me."

Cameron smirked, shook his head from side-to-side and then entertained the uncomfortable thought that Paul Kanner was winding him up in order to evade a beating. In one of the Personal, Social, Health and Economic Education classes he'd attended, he was told that kids with Asperger's rarely lied, told jokes or tried to fool people. He had assumed that Kanner was a 'full-aspie' and wouldn't be able to wind him up, but now he was beginning to wonder.

"You are joking Kanner! Can you even kick a ball?"

"I'm not good at jokes but I can kick a ball. Will you help me improve my skills?"

John Cameron smacked Paul Kanner's head 'playfully' and walked away. Paul felt curiously elated: maybe he should borrow more of Dr

Benjamin Zeigranik's psychological tactics!

Back at home, Paul went to his room immediately after supper with a sense of purpose. He'd felt better about himself than he'd felt for months and his interaction with Cameron made him feel that despite his social limitations, he could take charge of his own life. Bella appeared to be snoozing in the hallway, so he could now devote time to further researching Jericho Castle. But first, he would fire off an e-mail to Sgt Joe Bertolli. Paul's message was that he was concerned about all the incidents that had occurred at Jericho Castle and wondered whether he had time to meet to discuss the matter. Paul included his table of incidents, locations and explanations as an attachment to the e-mail.

Opening his search list from the night before, Paul began to look at the most recent entries on steps taken to improve the safety of Jericho Castle. Invariably, these were brief and dull accounts of structural improvements that had been planned or were currently in progress. One article mentioned that Old Heritage Holdings, the company that owned the castle, were in the process of recruiting additional security personnel.

Paul now turned his attention to the older entries, relating to the history of the castle and its construction. It turned out that the castle is relatively very new. Construction began on its site in Hertfordshire in 1873 and was completed in 1880. Its design was based on the original 11th century drawings for Arundel Castle in Sussex. Jericho Castle was the brainchild of Guy de Courcy, a wealthy London businessman who traced his family roots to the Norman nobleman, Roger de Montgomery, who had built Arundel Castle. Passionate about Norman history, de Courcy designed Jericho Castle allegedly to advance children's education. To this end, Jericho was essentially a scale-model of Arundel, occupying exactly half the land area occupied by the original. According to one article in *History Today* Jericho

Castle was also a vanity project: a great advertisement for de Courcy himself and his business ventures. Paul thought that this was all very interesting, but it shed no light whatsoever on the appalling safety record of the castle.

Just as Paul clicked on the next link, he received an e-mail alert. It was from Sgt Joe Bertolli. He opened Bertolli's e-mail and read that the sergeant found the tabulated incidents at Jericho Castle very interesting and could pop over to Paul's house in Bertram Street on Saturday morning if Paul was free. The sergeant's interest galvanised Paul's sense that he was onto something important. He replied immediately that Saturday would be great. The meeting would take place in two days and he really looked forward to it. Paul was now distracted with recollections of the case of 'Mr Sheen' in which he'd served as a key witness in helping the sergeant solve a very unusual serial burglary case. Paul was now reliving the sense of excitement he'd felt when he was involved in that case, and the glow that came from helping to finally solve it.

Paul's attention was dragged to the present moment by the next and more promising headline...

Is Jericho Castle a House of Secrets?

The author of the piece, which appeared in *Treasure Hunting Magazine*, outlined and passed judgement on three rumours concerning secret stashes hidden in the castle. One rumour claimed that a hitherto unknown part of the 8th Century *Lindisfarne Gospels* was hidden within the castle. The beautifully illuminated Anglo-Saxon manuscript of the New Testament gospels of Matthew, Mark, Luke and John were housed in the British Library in London. According to one historian, some additional loose pages were taken by the Vikings during their raid on Lindisfarne Monastery in AD793 and transported to Denmark. The historian further claimed that these pages were subsequently purchased on the black market by Guy de Courcy who had hidden them in the castle during its construction. Another story was that rogue archaeologists had more recently used the castle as a vault for their ill-gotten gains, including jewellery illegally recovered from ancient Egyptian tombs. Yet another more recent rumour concerned the Hatton Garden jewellery heist of 2015. This was hailed as one of the biggest burglaries in British history and was committed by a number of elderly, retired burglars. In the article, it was stated that some social media stories suggested that some of the stolen jewellery was hidden in Jericho Castle, sometime during the six-week period that the castle was undergoing scheduled repair work and was closed to the public. The author of the article concluded that there was no hard evidence for any of these rumours and that the people who had created these were motivated by a desire for public recognition.

Paul tugged on his hair for some seconds and shut down his laptop. He had a lot to discuss with Sgt Joe Bertolli on Saturday.

Chapter 4

Working at the Edges of a Puzzle

The white Ford Capri spluttered as it juddered to a halt outside 29 Bertram Street. Sergeant Joe Bertolli slid languidly from the driver's seat and coughed as if in sympathy with his aging car. Bertolli strode to the front door to be greeted by the yapping warning of Paul Kanner's dog Bella. Mrs Kanner opened the door and with a smile beckoned the detective inside the house.

"Paaauuul! Paauuul! Your policeman's here!"

"He'll only be a minute sergeant."

Paul Kanner ambled to the hallway and gave Sgt Bertolli an awkward smile. "Hello Joe...glad you could come. Um...nice to see you." Bertolli gave Paul a wry smile. He thought the boy's levels of self-assurance and social poise had improved significantly in the past few months. *Those chats that Paul had*

had with Dr Benjamin Zeigarnik must be paying off!

"Good to see you Paul. I gather you have a mystery for me to solve!" Paul's awkward smile spread to the rest of his body as he ambled to the garage with the detective following in his wake.

Hunched over a workbench, Paul and Joe examined a printout of the table of incidents that Paul had produced two days ago. Joe Bertolli agreed that the data were very alarming. "Well Paul, I must admit I am as puzzled as you are. It's been very dull at Greenwich Station of late, so when I received your e-mail, I began immediately to make some inquiries. I checked the National Crime Database and it seems that you are right: Hertfordshire Police only investigated two of the incidents: the dead teacher and the missing historian. I also checked with Hertfordshire County Council, who claimed that they were aware of each incident and had kept detailed records. The council was instrumental in getting Old Heritage Holdings to undertake repairs and other projects to improve the safety of Jericho Castle. I was also told by the council official that various education authorities had been warned to take extra precautions on school visits, including the national government's Department for Education and Employment. I also checked with English Heritage, the organisation that manages many castles, to find out how many accidents and other incidents typically occur in their castles. As you might already have guessed, the number and severity of the incidents at Jericho is well off the scale!"

Paul Kanner knit his brows and steeled himself to speak. "Erm...I read something else about Jericho Castle. There are rumours that people have hidden treasure or historical artefacts in there."

"Are the rumours about specific artefacts Paul?" Paul took out his mobile 'phone and googled the article in *Treasure Hunting Magazine.* He opened the link and handed his 'phone over to Joe Bertolli. Bertolli read the article in stunned silence. After a minute or so, he rubbed his eyes and sighed.

"How fantastical Paul! Why would anyone hide unknown bits of the *Lindisfarne Gospels*, or Egyptian tomb-treasure or modern-day jewellery in such a public place? I have to agree with the author: these rumours are just that...rumours!"

Paul's face assumed a glum expression as he met Bertolli's opinion with silence. He felt that the detective had been too dismissive. "So why are there so many unexplained accidents at the castle? Maybe they're not accidents after all. Maybe someone has caused these deliberately in some way. Maybe they want people to keep away from the castle."

Bertolli felt instinctively that Paul was barking up the wrong tree, but he didn't want to erode his new-found self-confidence. "OK Paul, let's look at this like a jigsaw puzzle and see what fits. Like my dad always used to say, it's best to start getting the edges of the puzzle together and then everything else falls into place. So, what are the "edges" of this particular problem?

Paul felt a sense of overwhelming confusion as he tried to grapple with Bertolli's jigsaw-puzzle metaphor. His obvious puzzlement was not lost on Joe Bertolli.

"Let me put it another way Paul. What evidence do we have that we can be sure about so that we can begin to see what kind of problem we have at Jericho Castle?"

"Well, one fact is that there have been many more accidents at Jericho Castle in the past five years than in other castles. Erm...another fact is that over one-third of these serious incidents came about through unknown causes. A third fact is that...er... the two cases investigated by the Hertfordshire Police are unresolved...the teacher who was crushed by falling masonry might have been...er... the victim of an intentional act for all we know. The historian who disappeared from the castle five years ago has still not been found. I don't know if this counts, but

I've also noticed that the two most serious cases...er... death and disappearance, involved the castle chapel. Something strange is definitely happening at Jericho Castle!"

Bertolli gazed at Paul uncertainly. Maybe Paul had a case...but it all seemed so bizarre and speculative. "Look Paul, you've made some good points and I can't dismiss the logic of your points. It just seems so improbable to me that if these incidents were caused by someone that they would go unnoticed for so many years. The castle does not fall under the jurisdiction of the Metropolitan Police so I don't have the power to investigate this directly: it should be a case for Hertfordshire Police... though we have been known to collaborate with them on other cases in the past. Let me think about this some more. In the meantime, maybe it would be a good idea to have a brainstorming session with Benjamin Zeigarnik...he always throws up something new, even if it's just the spaghetti he's just eaten." Bertolli shuffled his feet in embarrassment in response to the look of puzzlement on Paul's face.

Following Joe Bertolli's departure, Paul ambled up to his room and powered up his laptop. He was really looking forward to meeting up with Joe and Benjamin again, but in the meantime, he should try to dig a little deeper to find out whether anyone else had registered their suspicions about Jericho Castle. He decided to google "Jericho Castle chapel" and saw only one result that he hadn't seen before. As he clicked on the link, his eyes widened when he saw the title of the article:-

The Whispered Secrets of Castle Chapels: The Case of Jericho Castle

The article appeared in the *Journal of Medieval History* and was authored by Halva Halloumi, Professor of Medieval History at the University of Hertfordshire. The online publication showed that this article was uploaded only two days ago. Paul felt a tingling sensation along his spine as he began to read the densely-worded article. The article pointed out that for centuries, castle chapels were sites of special significance for hidden secrets. Rumours about valuable documents being hidden in a castle chapel had been kicking around since at least the 11th century. Historians researching diaries written centuries ago by monks, priests and noblemen often found references to rumours about castle chapels. Sometimes, these rumours turned out to be true. In fact, between the 11th and 14th centuries, a job as a castle priest (often called a chaplain) was particularly prized as it offered the prospect of uncovering treasure in the workplace! Professor Halloumi's own research uncovered letters and diaries concerning the chapel in Jericho Castle. Even though this was not a 'real' castle and was built relatively very recently, there were nonetheless a number of stories relating to it in the recovered diaries of three historians in 1905, 1929 and 1961, in a letter by the castle's chaplain (1956) and in a local politician's diary (1992). These five sources made a similar claim: that a valuable medieval manuscript of some sort had been hidden somewhere in the chapel of Jericho Castle. Professor Halloumi concluded her article by saying that her various attempts to obtain permission to investigate these claims had been met with blank refusal by the owners, Old Heritage Holdings. Her final sentence greatly amused Paul:

Let's see if Old Heritage Holdings can hold onto their old heritage when I ask all my historian and teacher friends to boycott the place!

Paul walked away from his desk and twirling his hair, paced the room. He had a lot to think about.

Chapter 5

Happy Gathering

In his haste, Sergeant Joe Bertolli almost gambolled down the steps of Greenwich Police Station as he raced to the station's car park. He was due to pick up Paul Kanner at 12.00 and it was already 12.13. He was beginning to think that it was time to avoid the police station on Saturday mornings as his few colleagues on the weekend shift were always particularly argumentative and grouchy. He had allowed himself to get involved in a pointless argument with three of his colleagues about the relative merits of Ford Capris and the newer Ford Mondeos and he was now running very late. As soon as he got into his car he called the Kanners' landline and texted Benjamin Zeigarnik with his excuses.

As he turned the ignition key, Bertolli's Capri

greeted him with a series of low whines, coughs and hiccups. Bertolli squeezed out of the car, stumbled towards the rear and gave one of the wheels an almighty kick. Scratching his head in frustration, he became aware of a faint cacophony of laughter. He felt his gaze drawn as if by a magnet to the second-floor windows of the police station. There, in a huddle, framed like a painting of three laughing cavaliers, were his colleagues, who were savouring Bertolli's misfortune and revelling in the indisputable evidence of the inferiority of the Ford Capri! This was turning out to be a bad day...a very bad day!

Bertolli made a conscious effort to blot out his odious gloating colleagues and put on his thinking hat. In this clearer state of mind he noticed something trailing out of the car's exhaust pipe. Bending down, Bertolli tugged at what appeared to be a piece of fabric. As he continued to pull, the fabric revealed itself to be a blue-and-white hooped football sock. He jumped into the driver's seat and turned the ignition key again. This time, the engine started after the usual mere three attempts and emitted only a tiny, just-audible splutter before it roared into life. He wound his window down and glared at his window-framed colleagues, who at this point were doubled-up and breathless with laughter. Bertolli gave them a threatening stare as he contemplated the various gruesome ways in which he would exact his revenge.

The almost-yellow white Ford Capri coughed to a halt just outside Paul Kanner's house at 29 Bertram Street. Joe Bertolli slid out of the car and ambled towards the gate. The front door opened before Bertolli had taken even a single step on the front path. Paul Kanner appeared extremely agitated.

Having appeased Paul with reminders of the glorious pizza that would be on offer at *Café Roma* in a little while, Bertolli set his sights on the seven-mile drive to Bloomsbury in central London, where he and Paul were scheduled to meet their friend, the psychologist Dr Benjamin Zeigarnik.

Joe Bertolli's Ford Capri behaved itself surprisingly well and completed the tortuous journey to Bloomsbury in a little over half an hour. Bertolli was now in a positive frame of mind as he steered the car to one of the remaining three empty parking spaces behind *Cafe Roma*. Paul also perked up as the smells of Italian cooking wafted toward him as he got out of the car.

As they made their way to the front of the restaurant, they caught a glimpse of Dr Benjamin Zeigarnik rushing from his metallic red Lambretta motor scooter towards the door of the restaurant. Bertolli smiled inwardly, for even though he and the police psychologist were firm friends, there had always been an element of competition in all of their shared undertakings. It was quite evident that Benjamin Zeigarnik was a driven and competitive man who did not enjoy being considered second-best.

Joe Bertolli opened the door for Paul and ushered him in. Benjamin Zeigarnik was already seated at his favourite window-seat, napkin at his throat, as he tucked into bread and olives. Hovering in attendance was the renowned chef and former lecturer in Roman history, Luigi Pecorino.

Benjamin and Luigi simultaneously greeted Joe and Paul as they approached the table. Benjamin had a twinkle in his eye and Luigi looked as happy as when he used to organise family meals in the old days. His warmth and fondness for human company led to him being a very popular lecturer and restaurateur, but even though he was never short of company, Luigi often looked back nostalgically to the days of love and laughter when he cooked for family members. Those days were now long-gone, but for the past thirty years he had regarded Benjamin as a son and always felt a special warmth and connection in his presence. In recent months, he felt as though he had acquired a new son and grandson in the shape of Joe Bertolli (who was of Italian heritage after all) and Paul Kanner (who loved Roman history).

Luigi brought menus to the table and asked them to shout out when they were ready to order. Retreating to his kitchen, Luigi began to wonder what this meeting of Benjamin, Joe and Paul was about. The previous time all three were here was to discuss the case of the mysterious "Mr Sheen", who it turned out had a very unusual motive for burgling so many places in South-East London. Well, he was sure to find out before long what the latest mystery was all about.

Benjamin called Luigi and the three collaborators made their order: pepperoni and mushroom pizza for Paul; spaghetti with clams for Joe and large rigatoni pasta with vodka sauce for Benjamin.

While they were waiting for their meals to arrive, Joe Bertolli set the wheels in motion. "So Benjamin, as I mentioned on the 'phone Paul believes something sinister has been going on at Jericho Castle these past five years." Paul Kanner felt the inquisitive gaze of both men as he tried to marshal his thoughts into a coherent account of the various strands of evidence he had come across.

"Well...er...the first thing was my classmate Lisa Khan falling from the castle rampart and being taken to hospital. It seemed strange that she should have fallen from there as there was a secure railing and unless she ran at the railing or was pushed I can't see how it could've happened. Then I started to search for information on the castle on the internet..." Paul pulled out a neatly folded copy of the incidents table that he had compiled and passed it over to Benjamin Zeigarnik.

Benjamin screwed up his eyes in concentration as the full force of the tabulated data hit him in the face. "*Bozhe moi*! My God, it cannot be! Paul, where did you get the data from?" Paul explained how he came by the incident reports on the internet. "I am speechless Paul. We must get these reports verified as a matter of urgency."

Joe Bertolli coughed and lifted his head up to gaze at Benjamin Zeigarnik. "I have already verified these incidents. The question really is whether they are the product of chance or of something more sinister."

Zeigarnik shook his head from side to side as if trying to negate the reality represented in Paul's tabulated incidents. Paul sheepishly looked at Joe with expectant eyes, seeking his permission to continue with his account. Joe nodded his approval.

"There's more strange stuff. Some stories about artefacts and manuscripts from the past being buried in the castle chapel. Even a rumour that the Hatton Gardens jewellery thieves stashed some valuables there. There's a history professor who says that for many centuries there have been stories concerning valuable documents being hidden in castle chapels. She says there have been accounts of a valuable medieval manuscript hidden in Jericho castle in the diaries of historians and other people."

Benjamin Zeigarnik cast a subtle glance at Joe Bertolli, not wanting Paul to feel in any way undermined. Bertolli answered with an almost imperceptible shrug of his shoulders. "My friends, I cannot understand how Jericho Castle could have remained open these past five years with such a dreadful health and safety record and with so many rumours...erm...stories doing the rounds. Surely, the Hertfordshire Police and Hertfordshire County Council must be aware of the incidents that have taken place. How has this place escaped proper scrutiny by the authorities?"

Paul felt very unqualified to deal with questions about political and bureaucratic institutions and looked to Joe Bertolli to answer. "Well Benjamin, both the police and the council have recorded the various incidents. The problem seems to be that the castle broadly complies with the relevant health and safety legislation. The owners, Old Heritage Holdings, were asked to increase the safety features of the castle, but these were deemed minor improvements, such as putting clear markings on steps and regularly checking the integrity of safety rails."

"But you would think head-teachers throughout the country must have heard about some of these accidents. Why are they allowing their kids to go there on school trips?" Before anyone could begin even thinking of a possible answer, Luigi waltzed to the table accompanying the waiter who brought their food.

"Luigi, this looks delicious. Why don't you join us and help us with our little conundrum?" Benjamin Zeigarnik filled in Luigi on the key points of their discussion while Paul and Joe guzzled their food with audible groans of pleasure.

"*Oh mio dio*! My God, this is much worse than I'd thought. Over the years I have heard some odd stories about strange incidents at Jericho Castle, but I didn't know there were so many cases. One of my friends told me that a colleague from his university, who was a medieval historian, disappeared some years ago, having last been seen at the castle."

Joe gazed at Luigi's puzzled face and addressed him slowly, trying to clarify his own thoughts on this mystery. "Luigi, I've consulted with Hertfordshire Police about the missing historian. His name was Dr Marcus Beard formerly of the University of Kent. There is absolutely no trace of the man. The officer I spoke to had been involved in the case and he let slip the unguarded comment that his disappearance was probably a scam...the disappearance was some kind of evasive manoeuvre, an attempt to defraud an insurance company or avoid paying some heavy duty debts. The case is still open but I sensed it has become a very cold case, even after only five years. Of course, Dr Beard, if he were alive, could be anywhere right now, so there's a limit to what any local police force can do. Tell me Luigi, have you heard any other stories from your historian friends?"

"Yes, now I remember! About a year ago, I came across an old friend who told me about an eccentric colleague of hers who was doing research on claims that castles were used as hiding places for valuable old manuscripts and artefacts. This historian...I forget her name now, is obsessed with the idea that castle chapels were considered as particularly safe hiding places and I seem to remember that she was looking into Jericho Castle as well."

"Halva Halloumi!" exclaimed Paul, Joe and Benjamin in unison. Such an unforgettable name for an author of an unforgettable article on castle chapels!

"Yes, that's it! How could I forget such a beautiful name? So you know of her?"

Paul Kanner pulled out his mobile 'phone as Luigi Pecarino screwed up his face in an uncharacteristic scowl of disapproval. Paul passed his 'phone to Luigi, who wasn't quite sure what to do with the offending object. "Look at the screen Luigi...it's Professor Halva Halloumi's article." Luigi's eyes widened and then his head nodded in recognition of what he was reading. While he had not read the article before, the ideas in it were familiar, as his friend had told him about her colleague Professor Halloumi's ideas.

The four companions sat in a daze around the table, each trying in his own way to make sense of the information that had been shared. After a few minutes, Joe Bertolli broke the silence. "In order for us to make any headway with this, we need to come up with possible explanations of these incidents. We keep coming back to the point that maybe nothing mysterious is going on, that all or most of these incidents are due to random misfortune. The point is, we can't uncover evidence for foul play unless we have some ideas about *why* these incidents have been caused and *how* they've been caused. Feeling super-creative after Luigi's delicious meal, I'd like to go all out with a sort of conspiracy theory. Someone has a valuable secret buried somewhere in Jericho Castle. If a visitor comes close to uncovering the secret, they are dealt with in various ways. The apparently random accidents are caused intentionally in some way to create a reputation that the castle is unsafe, so as to ward off curious snoops." Joe folded his hands on the table and gave a self-satisfied smile.

Benjamin Zeigarnik guffawed and shook his head. "Joe my friend, the whole point is that these "accidents" are not keeping people away and I wonder whether the notoriety of the place is fuelling interest from schools and others. Just think, you are a hard-working history teacher who only rarely gets to see a glimmer of interest in your students' eyes. So, for the school trip, you would like to generate some excitement. You're going to take them to this cool place where lots of un-cool things happen...how exciting! Of course, no one thinks the bad things will happen to them, especially teenagers. A winning formula: everyone wants to sign up for the visit to Jericho Castle and you have a teacher made happy by the enthusiasm of the students."

"Look Benjamin, are you trying to tell me that someone is *causing accidents* so that history teachers can have a nice day? That's a preposterous idea!"

Luigi looked at the two disputing men and decided it was time to chip in with his opinion before things became over-heated between Joe and Benjamin. "You know, both ideas are very plausible. Maybe the accidents have a deterrent effect in keeping some people away, especially people who might be tempted to snoop after-hours. At the same time, they may increase the attractiveness of the place for some people, especially during opening hours, when there is some level of security. If anyone

57

is behind these incidents, they may have hit upon the perfect formula of attracting customers during the day and putting off people whose visit is motivated by curiosity for treasure or secret manuscripts and what-have-you."

Joe and Benjamin wore appreciative smiles as they grasped the beauty and elegance of Luigi's formulation. Paul on the other hand wore a puzzled frown and narrowed his gaze at Luigi's bright-red tie. He mumbled a few words and got up to visit the toilet. The three men looked at each other in puzzlement. When Paul returned, Zeigarnik smiled warmly and asked Paul what he thought.

"Erm...well, I think the same as what I said before I went to the toilet. It must be the owners who are doing it. If Luigi is correct, then only the owners stand to gain from increased numbers of regular visitors and decreased numbers of treasure hunters."

The three adults around the table smiled

appreciatively at Paul. Even though nothing had been resolved definitively, Luigi's suggestion and Paul's deduction gave them an anchor for the mass of statistics, stories and rumours that had been bouncing between them around the dining table.

Chapter 6

Monday's Pickings

Paul Kanner awoke feeling exhausted. He hated Monday mornings and this particular Monday was promising to be a particularly bad day. He was awake half the night replaying Saturday's conversations round the table at *Café Roma.* The Jericho Castle mystery was rapidly becoming an obsession for Paul and sidelining all of his other projects. To make matters worse, he had agreed via e-mail to meet John Cameron for a lunch-time knock-about with a football. He couldn't really get out of this without inviting an intensification in hostilities. Cameron was going to humiliate him one way or another, but Paul knew he had to stick with the agreement in the hope that this display of "bottle" and "normality" would temper the contempt in which he was held by his school peers.

Just as Paul finally started on the hazardous journey from bed to slippers, Bella came bounding into his room like a crazed streak of lightning and started growling and tugging at his pyjama bottoms. Paul was often puzzled by Bella's erratic behaviour and often wondered why she was so annoyed in the mornings.

As Paul approached the entry gate of the school he noticed Mr Snow, the history teacher who had suffered a heart attack during the school trip to Jericho Castle. Paul started to wonder about the unfortunate Lisa Khan who had fallen from that terrible height. *Was it really an accident or was she pushed? Is she recovering well?* It was times like these that Paul felt keenly the absence of close friendships with his school peers. Sometimes, it helped to have someone with whom to share your enthusiasms and worries.

"Hello Mr Kanner, you look a little more distracted than usual this morning..."

"Er...good morning Mr Snow. I saw you and it reminded me of Jericho Castle and Lisa's accident. It's nice to see you back at school sir."

"Thank you Paul, it's good to be back. I hate nothing more than being under doctors' orders to rest. Yes, poor Lisa! I spoke to her parents a couple of days ago and it seems her physiotherapy and rehab therapy will continue for another couple of months or so. I feel very guilty about her accident. We took all the necessary precautions, but maybe I should have heeded some of the bad press about the place. Is she a particularly close friend of yours?"

"Er...not really. We talk sometimes but I don't know her that well. Erm...do you think Lisa's fall was really accidental sir?"

Mr Snow's eyes widened to a glare as he marched off leaving an emphatic "Yes!!!" ringing in Paul's ears. Paul had always liked Mr Snow who was usually very enthusiastic in his teaching and was also one of the gentler and kinder teachers. Paul was taken aback by Mr Snow's latest display. Maybe heart attacks did this to people.

~~~~~~~~~~

Meanwhile, in the bowels of Greenwich Police Station, Joe Bertolli was furiously twirling his hair in a state of frustrated indecision. He was desperate to resolve the Jericho Castle mystery but had no legal jurisdiction over this. Even if his boss DCI Sara Gravesham approved such an undertaking, he would be powerless to launch an investigation as the castle was in Hertfordshire Police's patch, not the Met's. What made matters worse was that he had no urgent official cases to work on that could serve as a distraction. He'd be a lot happier if he could convince himself that there really was something sinister going on at the castle and that the incidents there weren't just random or accidental events.

Stewing in his self-contained misery, Bertolli

was suddenly brought to the present moment by the dramatic entrance of Detective Constable Maxine Carter, who was yielding a samurai sword.

"Hi Joe, how goes it? Got this for a fancy-dress party I'm going to tonight. Don't worry, the sword is just a theatre prop and has no cutting edge."

Maxine Carter was one of the very few colleagues that Joe Bertolli got along with. She was an extremely bright maths graduate who joined the police so that she could satisfy the more adventurous part of her personality. As it happened, she spent most of her time in the open-plan detectives' office at the station staring into a computer screen. She was, after all, the station's chief geek and number cruncher.

Seeing Maxine with her sword triggered a thought in Joe. "Hey Maxine, I wonder if you can help me out a bit. I have a mega problem for your big brain."

Maxine patiently listened as Joe recounted in

detail what he had learned about the mysterious incidents at the castle and his concerns about not being able to investigate the place to establish whether anything sinister was going on. "The only helpful thing I can suggest now is to check whether at least one of the two most serious cases – the person who went missing or the person who died was a London resident. You might then be able to persuade the boss that a new collaborative investigation with Hertfordshire police is called for. You'd then have an excuse to go up there and scratch around in Jericho Castle to see if you found anything interesting."

"Nice idea Maxine. I've learned that the missing historian, Dr Marcus Beard, was based at the University of Kent in Canterbury. It seems unlikely that he commuted fifty miles or more from London each day, so I doubt that he'd lived in London at the time of his disappearance. As for the teacher who died at the castle, the coroner's report gives no cause for reopening the case: the man was crushed to death by falling masonry – seemingly an unfortunate accident probably caused by parts of the chapel ceiling becoming structurally unsound over the years. In any event, these are fairly cold cases, so I'm not sure that I can persuade the boss to re-open an investigation, even if there were a London connection."

"OK Joe, let's find a different angle. From what you've told me, quite a few of the accident victims were kids on a school trip to the castle. Given that the latest victim was from one of our local schools here in Greenwich, can't we persuade DCI Gravesham to authorise a short investigation of the castle to rule out foul play? After all, there was no clear-cut explanation for Lisa Khan's fall from a twenty-foot-high wall that appeared safe and secure to witnesses, including your friend Paul Kanner."

Joe Bertolli rather unexpectedly smiled as he gazed at Maxine twirling her pretend-sword. "You said 'we'...it sounds as though you want to get involved in solving this mystery!"

"You know me Joe, I love adventures and it's time I spent a bit of time away from my office computer. You know, the more I think about it the more I realise that DCI Gravesham will not on any account authorise an investigation into Jericho Castle. Maybe we need to visit the place as customers and do a bit of unofficial snooping. Are you doing anything this Saturday? I think I can do a bit of online digging that might help us know where to look for clues."

With a glint in his eye, Joe Bertolli bobbed his head in agreement..."You're on the case. Let's do it!"

~~~~~~~~~~

It was a frustrating Monday for another individual who had been trying to make sense of the incidents at Jericho Castle. Dr Benjamin Zeigarnik paced around his lab in Senate House like a caged animal. He spent the early part of the morning going round in circles thinking about Saturday's discussions at Luigi's restaurant. Try as he might, he could not settle on a consistent explanation for these thirty-odd incidents. Was Luigi right in thinking that there was some sinister strategic intelligence behind these events? Or maybe it was just a set of random and unrelated unfortunate events.

To make matters worse, the experiments that he had scheduled for today had been blighted by a combination of equipment failure and unreliable research participants who had failed to show up. Benjamin was fuming! He fought to resist the temptation to cool his heels in the aromatic warmth of *Café Roma* and instead contented himself with the shop-bought sandwich that he had picked up this morning.

Dismantling the ridiculous packaging in which the sandwich was entombed, Benjamin stared at the contents with evident disdain. Funny how sandwich fillings can be made to appear more nutritious and tasty than they really are. Tiny slithers of tomato appearing at the cut edges of the sandwich, or thick succulent slices of ham, turn out to be mere window dressing. When you lift the top slice of bread, you soon see that the interior of the sandwich has no tomatoes and the ham is very thin! An illusion that fools us and sets up optimistic expectations about what we are about to eat...maybe a bit like Jericho Castle. What kind of illusions might have been created there? With that thought, Benjamin scribbled a hasty note in his notebook and tossed the remnants of the sandwich into the bin.

~~~~~~~~~~

An uncharacteristically morose Luigi Pecorino spent this particular Monday morning staring into space as his body slumped over the kitchen worktop. He had spent much of the previous night churning things over in his mind and when he finally got to sleep, was assailed by dark dreams of being chained to the walls of a castle dungeon. As a former historian, he had encountered a few stories about Jericho Castle, but the full force of Saturday's revelations in this very restaurant had thrown his mind into a spin. He felt an urge to do something to help him get to the bottom of this mystery. He was too old to go clambering over castle battlements in search of clues, but maybe he could use his brain instead.

One thing that had particularly struck him was the young Paul Kanner's throw-away comment at the end of Saturday's meal: the owners of Jericho Castle are the ones who might be gaining from all these incidents and it would make sense that they might be causing them. Yesterday, Luigi had read carefully the article by Halva Halloumi that Paul Kanner had shown him. At the end of her article, Professor

Halloumi had made some sarcastic comments about the owners of the castle, Old Heritage Holdings. Maybe she knew more than she could reveal in her article. Maybe he could talk to her... after all, she is a colleague of one of his friends.

~~~~~~~~~~

Paul Kanner's Monday was about to get much worse at the approach of lunch-time. He was due to meet John Cameron in a few minutes and have a knock-about with the ball. Even though their last lengthy encounter went quite well, Paul felt an instinctive tightening of his chest whenever he thought of this erstwhile bully. Before he even reached the enclosed tarmac football pitch, his worst fears were confirmed as he found himself on the ground as a ball careened from the side of his face and into the grinning arms of John Cameron.

"Come on fool, ready for more practice? Try to

hit it with the other side of your face this time!"

Paul lay motionless and tried to buy a little time to fine-tune his response. He remembered what Dr Benjamin Zeigarnik had told him about bullies: *they like to feel superior by scaring and humiliating others; don't show fear or embarrassment and eventually they'll leave you alone. If they won't leave you alone, find a way of making them feel good about themselves that doesn't involve you being used as a target. If all else fails, make them laugh. Dr Zeigarnik said laughter is incompatible with violence. It was easy for him to say that, but Paul simply could not predict what would make people laugh and what would make them fly into a rage.*

Springing to his feet, Paul put on his best fake smile and gazed directly at Cameron's nose. "Like I said John, I do need the practice. If you're really good at coaching, I might even learn how to head the ball. By the way, my name is Paul and I'm no fool."

Cameron smirked and twirling the ball on his

index finger, led the way to the football pitch. Paul followed taking lively steps to keep up but inwardly crawling towards the football pitch. Unsurprisingly, Cameron's usual cronies were already strutting on the pitch. Cameron stared at Paul, placed the ball on the ground and gently kicked it along the ground towards Paul. "OK Paul, let's do some basics."

Chapter 7

Snoop Time

Barely able to suppress the next yawn, Joe Bertolli pulled up to the forecourt of Greenwich Police Station and inched his way out of the Capri. He hated early mornings, especially of the wet Saturday variety. Maxine Carter was already waiting for him in her snazzy metallic green Citroén C4. Bertolli glanced at his watch: 08.12...twelve minutes late. He entered the C4, mumbled an apology and strapped himself into this luxurious car. The engine barely made a sound when Maxine turned the ignition key and it purred like a kitten as it wove gracefully through the streets of Greenwich. Joe cast an appreciative eye at the car interior and was happy that he could almost stretch his legs in this roomy car: it wasn't always easy being 6'4".

The car gently halted outside 29 Bertram Street and Joe jumped out, ran to the front door and rang the bell. A forlorn Mrs Kanner opened the door and called out Paul's name. Bella came dashing down the stairs and into Joe Bertolli's arms, with Paul in her wake. Paul was finally going to get a full day to explore Jericho Castle.

The forty-mile drive to Jericho Castle passed without incident as Bertolli caught up on some beauty sleep and Paul revisited in his mind his previous visit there. Reimagining the prostrate body of Lisa Khan and the collapsing form of Mr Snow did little to alleviate Paul's anxieties about this dangerous place. To counteract these awful images, Paul reminded himself in a whisper to check out the chapel. It was Maxine's idea that the three of them should go to the castle together as a 'family group'. Hopefully, this would create the illusion of an innocent family outing and dispel any suspicions from prying eyes as they snooped around for any clues.

Having parked the car, Maxine Carter sprinted to the ticket booth and bought a family ticket which gave them a full-day's access to the castle and its surrounding gardens.

Maxine, Joe and Paul entered through the raised portcullis and blinked at each other in the semi-darkness. Joe was struggling with the idea that he had to play the role of a dad and Maxine was struggling with the idea that this castle was the setting for so many mishaps. Eventually, it was Paul who had taken the initiative and led the way to the area of the bailey where Lisa Khan had fallen.

Paul's furrowed brow and quivering features alerted Joe and Maxine to the distress he was experiencing, and it didn't take two detectives to figure out that this must be the place where Lisa Khan had fallen.

Keeping a little distance, Joe Bertolli gently tapped Paul on his back and spoke to him in a low voice. "Paul, we'll get soaked hanging around here. Let's go someplace where there's cover. I know that you were particularly interested in seeing the chapel and I'd really like to take a look at the castle keep, which I read houses a small museum of architectural drawings of various English castles." Paul's gaze continued to be transfixed by the spot where Lisa Khan had fallen during that fateful school-trip and he barely acknowledged Joe's presence. Maxine gestured to Joe and led   him a little distance away so as to allow Paul a little time to get himself back to the present moment.

Paul's head turned very slowly toward Joe and Maxine and his eyes widened as if in surprise. "I saw it again...the way Lisa lay there. She was quite far from the rampart wall when she was lying there...about three metres away. No one moved her and she couldn't have rolled such a distance. How did she fall so far away from the wall if she fell from the wall?"

Maxine smiled wryly to herself and wondered whether this boy's emotions were playing havoc with his imagination and memory. Composing herself so as not to appear too sceptical, she offered Paul a wine-gum and attempted to engage him in what was meant to appear as casual conversation. "Joe has mentioned on numerous occasions the last case you helped him with and you know he sees you as a very smart young man. He couldn't have solved that case without you. He also tells me that you're into science...so I wonder how a body can land by as much as three metres away from *that* wall?"

Paul focused on Maxine's chin as he struggled to formulate a comprehensive reply. "I think there are two possibilities: a body is propelled forward with a lot of force before it begins to fall...or a body is levered over the edge...erm...over the railing."

Impressed with the clarity of his answer, Maxine was nonetheless confident that Paul was allowing his imagination to run away with itself.

78

"Excellent Paul, you know your physics. Which of these two possibilities do you think applies to this case?"

Paul was beginning to feel as though he was back at school where every question from a teacher felt like a trap. Maxine had been quite nice, but he was beginning to sense that there was something behind her question that he couldn't quite grasp. "I don't know" mumbled Paul, his face a picture of bewilderment. *Was he supposed to know?*

Maxine cast a quick and furtive glance at Joe, who thought it was time to rescue the situation from turning into a sullen stalemate. "Paul, I'd really like to know what you think happened to Lisa?"

"Maybe she was pushed" was Paul's surly reply. "In case you think I have it wrong about where Lisa landed, I can tell you that I noticed where she fell because her body was roughly in line with that water-well. After the ambulance took Lisa and Mr Snow away, I noticed one of the uniformed castle security guards walked from the water-well to the wall and I counted four paces, which is about three metres."

An intrigued Joe Bertolli asked the very question that was guaranteed to flummox Paul: "*Why* did the security guard walk to the wall Paul?"

Paul's predictable response arrived after a whole minute of grimacing puzzlement, "I don't know."

As Paul turned and headed in the direction of the chapel, Maxine Carter whispered to Joe Bertolli: "Was she pushed or did she jump? She couldn't have just fallen over that safety rail."

The chapel door resisted Paul's efforts but he finally managed to get it to creak open. He was followed into the dark interior by Maxine and Joe, who were on full alert in this spooky atmosphere. Paul strode along the dimly lit nave running down the centre and halted at the apse at the far end of the chapel where a giant crucifix sat atop an intricately carved wooden structure.

Paul bent down to peer into the lattice-work of the wooden structure in the hope of uncovering any hint of something being secreted there. Just as he began to poke around, the door behind them creaked again and a slightly hunched moustachioed man in a uniform hovered for a few seconds. Joe Bertolli casually ambled up to the security guard and quietly reassured him that they were just having a look-around. Before leaving without uttering a single word, the man pointed a finger at a sign on the lattice-work that read: PLEASE DO NOT TOUCH ANY PART OF THIS STRUCTURE.

Paul turned and walked toward Joe and Maxine, who at this point faced the closed door. "It's him. That's the guard who walked four paces to the wall after Lisa Khan fell. I noticed him because he dragged one leg...erm... like he had a limp."

Maxine gave Joe Bertolli a quick glance. "Do you think he followed us in here Joe? Do you think that perhaps he recognised Paul as one of the kids who was here when Lisa fell?" Joe gently shook his head from side to side and led the way back along the nave to the door.

Once outside, the three companions sighed with relief at being out in the fresh air, even though it was still raining. The chapel was quite spooky, doubtless due to a combination of poor lighting, minimal ventilation and creaking sounds. Each of them realised that even if anything of value were hidden in the apse, it would take considerably more than curious visiting tourists to uncover it. Joe consulted the tourist map of the castle and suggested that they visit the dungeon as they had already survived one spooky experience. Paul looked beseechingly at Joe and agitatedly pointed out that there had been no mishaps reported in the dungeon, so they'd be best served looking elsewhere for clues.

Smiling in acknowledgement of Paul's unexpected show of assertiveness, Joe said "You have a point there Paul. Why don't you and Maxine plan the rest of our tour. Hopefully, we'll have better luck snooping around the other areas."

Ascending the steps that led to the castle rampart from which Lisa had fallen, Maxine reflected on the safety of the structure. The steps that they were climbing seemed sturdy and evenly spaced, with a solid hand-rail to grip for support. Looking above her head, she noticed that the edge of the rampart was secured by a solid-looking railing and a wire-mesh fence attached to the ground with large bolts. From this vantage point, it all seemed safe and secure; not a likely location for the kind of mishap that befell Lisa. She made a mental note to examine these safety features more closely when she got to the top.

Joe Bertolli was on the same wavelength as Maxine Carter, and both could very soon be seen engaging in experimental assaults of various kinds on the railing to test its safety. While Maxine tugged at the mesh fence, Paul stood at the battlements staring outwardly through one of the gaping crenels. He turned slowly to face Maxine and Joe.

"I don't like it here. Can we go soon?"

Joe spotted the security guard they'd seen in the chapel now down in the bailey. He realised that the man had probably been looking at them and now confirmed his guilt by hurriedly turning his head and walking away. *Was he actually spying on them?*

They left forty minutes later having made a whistle-stop tour of the castle keep, one watchtower and the barbican. The visit had left each of them with a deep sense of foreboding as they drove back to London in silence.

Chapter 8

Illusory Castle

Tuesday was almost always Benjamin Zeigarnik's favourite day of the week. He had no commitments to the university or the police and always kept this day free of social engagements. It was his day for thinking...*blue skies thinking* he would call it...to think freely about big topics in psychology without any pressure to come up with useful answers. He would tuck himself away in the study of his Camden flat, coffee percolator purring away, with a notepad and pen the only adornments to his desk.

But this particular Tuesday was very different. Benjamin had slept badly the previous two nights, struggling to come up with explanations for what was going on at Jericho Castle. He was deeply troubled by the sheer scale of the mishaps but also felt inadequate. Usually, he was able to proffer Joe Bertolli a psychological angle or two on a case which often helped. In this case, it was hard to come up with anything, except for yesterday's idea, now staring at him on his notepad, that packaged sandwiches were really a form of visual illusion. Maybe Jericho Castle was a bit like a shop-bought sandwich!

Dr Zeigarnik gruffly shook his head, walked to one of his over-burdened bookcases and picked up a book: *Eye and Brain*, by the famous psychologist Richard Gregory. He gazed at the book cover in fond reverie, recalling his early days as a lecturer when he used to teach about visual illusions. He smiled at the memory of reading several exam scripts where students had referred to the book as *Iron Brain*. Clearly these charlatans had not even bothered to set eyes on the book let alone read it! They simply relied on his spoken words during a lecture for the title of this famous book.

Flicking through the pages of the book, he slowed down as he approached the final chapters containing pictures of illusions. His eyes alighted on a famous illusion created by the American Psychologist Adelbert Ames. This was known as the Distorted Room.

The two girls in the picture are actually the same height! How is the one on the right made to appear like a giant? Adelbert Ames created some very strange rooms that looked normal to someone looking in through a small peephole. Even though the far-side wall was at an angle and sloped downward to the right, the viewer saw it as a normal square room. The person on the right seems taller because s/he is closer to the viewer and is as tall as the wall. Over the years, many people have created their own versions of the Distorted Room and taken photos through a peephole.

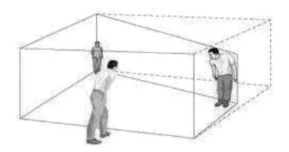

Tugging distractedly at his beard, Benjamin Zeigarnik continued to stare at the illusion on the page until he lost all focus and his vision became blurred. He started to recall that this illusion had been used in a number of movies, including the original version of *Charlie and the Chocolate Factory* in 1971. It was used to great effect in the *Lord of the Rings* movies to make Frodo Baggins and other hobbits appear suitably small, as well as in the *Harry Potter* movies to give Hagrid the appearance of a giant.

Could such distortions have been incorporated recently into renovations of key parts of the castle? How might this illusion be used to cause the kinds of mishaps that young Paul Kanner had documented? Zeigarnik drummed his desk with the pen, willing his ideas to come to life. Maybe the illusion could be used to make some of the castle's visitors running scared. Maybe if they looked where they shouldn't they would experience an illusion of something unusually big...monstrous even. Paul had mentioned that there were rumours of hidden treasures and manuscripts...perhaps the places where they are hidden were built like small distortion rooms. You have a peep, but see some gigantic scary object on the right and miss what is hidden on the left.

A self-satisfied smile played on Zeigarnik's lips as he turned his attention to the practical matter of testing his idea. He reached out for the laptop that was snoozing on the armchair in a back corner of his study and with a swipe of his finger, set the whirring intelligence to work. Consulting *Google Maps* revealed that the nearest railway station to Jericho Castle was St. Albans. He could catch the 12.53 train from Kentish Town Station and be in St. Albans for 13.22. The castle was only a short bus-ride away from St. Albans, so if he set off now, he could spend an unhurried afternoon exploring the castle.

As he quickened his pace toward the portcullis of Jericho Castle, Benjamin Zeigarnik was alerted by a sudden movement in the periphery of his vision. Turning his head quickly to the right, he caught the icy stare of a man in uniform and peaked cap. He looked like a policeman from this distance, but Zeigarnik reasoned that he must be some kind of security guard. The man continued to stare as he tweaked his over-size moustache. The guard seemed to be a man with a mission. The intensity of his stare convinced Zeigarnik that he was the sole object of concern for this curious moustachioed man. Not missing a beat, Zeigarnik marched purposefully under the portcullis gate and through to the ticket booth. When he turned his gaze back toward the portcullis, the security guard had disappeared.

Consulting the map in the little tour-guide that he was given with his entry ticket, Zeigarnik headed straight for the chapel. As he gazed at the stained-glass windows at the side of the chapel, he was overcome by a flood of youthful memories. During his very short military career in Russia, he had often marvelled at the ornate beauty of the Orthodox churches and cathedrals that he had been ordered to keep an eye on. At the time, people opposed to the Soviet government would often hold clandestine meetings in churchyards and he had been one of the many operatives who was spying on these "traitors". Truth be told, he was far too taken by the church windows to attend to his spying duties. These windows often depicted a notable saint embroiled in some miraculous happening or other which called to mind some of the fabulous stories that his grandmother had whispered to him at bedtime.

Snapping out of his reverie, Zeigarnik walked to the chapel entrance and pushed open the creaking door. Scanning all four corners of the chapel interior, he walked briskly along the nave and stopped at the apse. Zeigarnik had the same experience here as Paul Kanner, Joe Bertolli and Maxine Carter, who unbeknownst to him, had visited the castle on the previous day.

Bending down to examine the latticed structure in front of the giant crucifix, Zeigarnik's gleeful expression was suddenly frozen by the sound of the creaking door behind him. Turning his head slowly, he saw the unwelcome sight of the moustachioed security guard, who with a steely gaze walked up to Zeigarnik and pointed to a sign: PLEASE DO NOT TOUCH ANY PART OF THIS STRUCTURE. Before Zeigarnik could react, the guard turned on his heels and slowly walked away.

Benjamin Zeigarnik was not the sort of person who followed rules. He bent down once again and tried to peer through the lattice-work to see if he could make out whether anything was hidden there. His mobile-phone torch failed to illuminate matters and with a grunt of disappointment, he stretched to his full height and tugged at his beard. Roaming around the chapel for other promising targets, his eyes settled on the seating pews.

Systematically testing each pew by means of a hefty kick, Benjamin Zeigarnik reached the conclusion that all eight of these were solid and had

93

no hidden cavities in which anything could be hidden. Shaking his head in frustration and disgust, he slowly ambled up to the door, momentarily checking his map for directions to the nearest rampart stairway.

As the door creaked open, Zeigarnik caught a brief glimpse of something dark streaking across his peripheral vision. By the time he emerged from the doorway there was no sign of anyone.

Ascending the wooden stairway to the rampart, Benjamin Zeigarnik began to entertain doubts about his little quest. He recalled that Paul Kanner's classmate had fallen from one of the ramparts and a number of previous visitors had sustained injuries there. The ramparts are obviously worthy of investigation, but how might this relate to a Distorted Room? After all, the rampart was just a footpath alongside a high wall. As he reached the top of the stairs he caught sight of a tower wall at the far end of the rampart. Of course, maybe part of the watchtower was constructed as a Distorted Room! This thought brought Zeigarnik renewed vigour and a smile of anticipation which all too quickly were supplanted by a black void as the lumbering psychologist lay unconscious on the ground.

Chapter 9

A Recipe for Success

A sleep-deprived Luigi Pecorino stared wanly into his telescoped shaving mirror trying to remember why he had extended the mirror in the first place. The fact that he usually shaved every day seemed momentarily to have escaped him. His eyes glazing over as his mind entered a trance-like state, Luigi pulled himself out of the morass of confusion with one thought: *strong black espresso coffee and Amaretto biscotti!* He liked to dip these very hard biscuits into his coffee until they softened to the consistency of a very moist cake.

Shuffling to his private kitchen, which was immediately above his restaurant, *Café Roma*, Luigi Pecorino made himself an extra-strong espresso and fished out the *biscotti* from the top cupboard. Waves of clarity pulsed through his brain with each sip of coffee and each munch of *biscotti*. Within minutes normal service was resumed in Luigi's brain and he returned to a normal state of consciousness...which in Luigi's case, often included talking out loud to himself as if the larger-than-life chef and former historian was made up of two personalities. Since his wife Precious went on a pan-African tour four months ago, this tendency to hold conversations with himself had become a more frequent feature of Luigi's life.

"Okay, you've had coffee and *biscotti* and it's time to get down to business my friend!"

"Will you stop haranguing me for God's sake? I'm thinking!"

"Thinking, thinking, thinking! DO *something!*"

Dr Luigi Pecorino slammed his fist on the breakfast table, winced with pain and marched purposefully into the adjoining room which served as his study. He turned on his desktop, wiped crumbs from his mouth and went on a five-minute search for his very old Nokia 'phone, which he found nestled in an armchair beneath a pile of history magazines. He found Professor Halva Halloumi's website at the University of Hertfordshire and entered her 'phone number and e-mail address into his contacts list.

Stabbing his thumb on the number, he heard a woman's voice on the other end of the line.

"Halloumi speaking! Who is it?"

"Hello Professor Halloumi. My name is Luigi Pecorino. I am a close friend of your colleague Dr Adwoma Osei."

"Ah yes, Adwoma is a dear colleague. By the way, are you the Luigi Pecorino who wrote *Roman Foodlore*?"

"Yes, I am!" Luigi sounded more confident than he'd felt, for even though his book had won many awards, academic historians were notoriously critical of one another. His sense that the professor had had a drink or two made him even more wary.

"A very fine book indeed..er...Luigi."

"Well thank you...eh...Halva!"

Having got off to such a fine start, Luigi wasted no time in assailing Professor Halloumi with his pet theory about Jericho Castle. He told the professor that he had read her article about Jericho Castle and sensed that she had more things to say about the current owners, Old Heritage Holdings. He quickly added that he believed the owners were intentionally causing "accidents" in part to attract visitors to the castle.

Halva Halloumi was silent for some seconds as she tried to decide how much of her own speculative thinking she could safely disclose to this man whom she'd never met. "Nothing would surprise me! Old Heritage Holdings comprises three very crooked individuals: Julia Perkins, a former student of mine; Patrick Leyton, a disgraced banker; and Victoria Singh, a former archaeologist for the county of Somerset. They had all met as university students and encouraged each other in their nefarious ways.

Perkins was sacked from the British Museum for illegally selling various artefacts she'd stolen from the underground storage rooms and also served an eighteen-month prison sentence. Leyton was charged with hacking into his own customers' accounts and siphoning off funds into his friends' accounts. The court returned a verdict of "not guilty", but anyone who knows him knows he did it. The money he embezzled was probably used to finance Old Heritage Holdings' acquisition of Jericho Castle. Singh was accused of taking bribes from building contractors for forging inspection reports which resulted in the destruction of old Saxon burial grounds. They are an unsavoury lot Luigi and...dangerous, I think. I heard from a friend of mine that Jericho Castle was in a very bad state of disrepair when these three miscreants bought it, so they had little competition. English Heritage did not think it worth their while to invest millions into restoring what essentially is a mock-up of a castle."

"What about the stories you mentioned in your article Halva? Do you think that the castle chapel is really a hiding place for valuable manuscripts?"

"I really don't know Luigi. Of course, I've visited as a regular tourist, but everything is under tight wraps. I've written on a number of occasions requesting permission from Old Heritage Holdings to grant me access for research purposes and I always get the same negative reply, signed by my lovely former student, Julia Perkins!"

Luigi Pecorino scratched his head as his agitation reached new heights. "But shouldn't we go to the police or the county council with all this information?"

"Believe me I have, but Hertfordshire Police and the council both say the same thing: they don't have enough hard evidence to warrant an investigation. But one thing I saw on my third visit to the castle has given me food for thought. On the northern rampart, I..."

After ten seconds of silence, alarm bells began to ring in Luigi's head. "Halva! Halva! Are you there?" The line was dead.

Chapter 10

A Gaggle of Ideas

Friday afternoons at Hollenbeck High were always particularly highly charged. The kids were itching to kick off the weekend, the teachers were desperately trying to prevent their classes from dissolving into anarchy and the head-teacher was working over-time to whittle down the long queue of referred students. As much as he differed from the other kids, Paul Kanner was just as desperate for the school day to end.

The last two periods were dragging by slowly and Paul found himself thinking about tomorrow's gathering with Joe Bertolli, Benjamin Zeigarnik, Maxine Carter and Luigi Pecorino. He was so glad that he now had this "other life" away from the insecurities of the school environment.

"Mr Kanner! Will you please grace us with your

analysis of why rivers tend to flow in a southerly direction?" Ms Cooper, the geography teacher was one of Paul's more irksome teachers. She only ever asked Paul a question when she knew he'd be unable to answer because he hadn't been paying attention. Why didn't she ask him a question when he had been attentive? What was the point of her questions anyway?

"Erm...I think..." Paul's mind went blank. In these situations he found himself unable to answer a question even if he knew the answer.

"I'm not sure you do Mr Kanner!" Ms Cooper's riposte was met by guffaws and exaggerated laughter by the class, clearly aimed at further unsettling Paul, whose gaze wavered towards the middle distance. Still trying to shut out the disturbing cacophony of demented laughter and taunts, Paul turned sharply in the direction of John Cameron, who was seated two rows behind him and to his left. Cameron was out of his seat hooting and pointing an accusing finger at Paul, in case anyone in the class remained uncertain that Paul Kanner was the butt of this round of ridicule. Paul caught Cameron's eye, winked at him in a conspiratorial manner and then put on his best fake smile. John Cameron was stunned into silence.

These tricks that Dr Benjamin Zeigarnik had taught Paul seemed to be working for now, but Paul wondered how long he could keep up the pretence. He found it very difficult to act in a way that was different from how he felt. He was also worried that he was spending too much time pandering to Cameron and his cronies and not enough time thinking about his pet projects. Still, he hadn't been punched or badly abused for quite a while and maybe it was all worthwhile.

As soon as Paul got home, he ran up the stairs to his room, with Bella hot on his heels. He spent an obligatory fifteen minutes play-fighting with Bella, then gave her a rawhide strip to chomp on. This was the only reliable method of getting Bella to calm down so that Paul could think.

Paul was really looking forward to meeting the others for lunch tomorrow. Joe Bertolli had sent e-mails to arrange tomorrow's gathering, where it was hoped they would come up with fruitful avenues for solving the Jericho Castle mystery. Paul couldn't help but think that their previous discussions a week ago were missing something important, though he couldn't quite put his finger on exactly what this was.

~~~~~~~~~~

An unkempt and lethargic Joe Bertolli squeezed out of the white Ford Capri and ambled to the front gate of 29 Bertram Street. He battled with the gate latch, part of which came off in his hand, and took four long strides to the front door, which opened just as he got there. Mr Kanner smiled weakly as his eyes registered the dull metal clasp cradled in Bertolli's hands.

"Hello Mr Kanner. Er...sorry about this...just came off in my hands. I'll pay for a replacement."

"Don't worry Sergeant. It's happened to me before. I'll get Paul for you."

Paul came bounding out of the door with Bella snapping at his heels. "No Bella, go inside. Go on!" Paul dug out a treat from his pocket and tossed it into the depths of the hallway and quickly slammed the front door shut. "Hi Joe."

"Hi Paul! Ready for Chinese noodles?"

Paul beamed as he entered through the front passenger door of the Capri. Within ten minutes they were seated at the *Tai Won Mein* noodle bar in the centre of Greenwich. They were greeted profusely by Benjamin Zeigarnik and more demurely by Maxine Carter.

Joe Bertolli's eyes narrowed momentarily. "Where's Luigi?"

Before anyone could answer, a red-faced and

slightly tense Luigi Pecorino charged through the door and barrelled down the aisle towards them.

"Excuse me everyone. So good to see you all my friends. Phew, I thought I wouldn't make it here at all!"

Benjamin turned a very concerned face toward Luigi. "What's the matter Luigi? Is everything alright?"

"Everything is fine now. I was very worried about Professor Halva Halloumi. I called her for a chat on Tuesday and before we finished our conversation her line went dead. I've been calling four or five times a day since and only just managed to speak to her an hour ago. It turns out that her office 'phone at the university has had an intermittent problem. Oddly, this happened when I thought she was about to tell me something significant about Jericho Castle, which raised my suspicions of foul play at the time."

Joe detected continued concern in Luigi's voice

and expression. "Is Professor Halloumi OK Luigi?"

"I...think so. But...she sounded anxious when she spoke to me today. Maybe it's coincidence. Maybe I'll call her again another day..."

The five companions looked at their menus and each chose a fried noodle dish. The short wait for the food was spent with everyone in turn making various attempts to initiate conversations with Paul, who seemed a little flushed and anxious.

With food-laden plates in front of them, Joe Bertolli tried to impose an agenda and some sense of order. It was all too evident that his four companions were fully immersed in the scrumptious fare before them. "So...it would be good if we can all brief each other on what we're thinking about Jericho Castle. Erm, who would like to start?"

Joe Bertolli had grown used to being sidelined by his police colleagues, but on this occasion he was taken aback by the absence of any response from his companions. *Damned good noodles. Should have*

gone to one of the other places in Greenwich that
served less tasty food.

Finally, a response from Benjamin. "I hate cold noodles Joe...let's just eat first and talk later. The place is unusually quiet, so I'm sure we can order a drink or two after we've eaten and then have our discussion."

Joe and Benjamin were the first to finish their meals and engaged in small-talk whilst waiting for the others. Joe quickly scanned the faces of his companions and coughed lightly to attract everyone's attention.

"OK then. I'll kick off with what we discovered at Jericho Castle. As you'll all know from my e-mails, Maxine, Paul and I paid a visit as "regular visitors" on Tuesday. I rather suspect that our family act did not convince everyone there and certainly aroused the suspicions of one of the guards...a moustachioed fellow who belonged on the set of an old horror movie. His seemed to follow our every move. His peculiar behaviour convinces me that something truly suspicious is going on there. Maxine, Paul...anything to add?"

Paul reddened and looked intently at the dining table. Maxine gazed at him, then at Joe and spoke up. "We also checked out the rampart from which Paul's classmate Lisa Khan had fallen. No clues there. I agree with Joe: that guard was very suspicious and obviously thought we were snooping for something. I think he or his superiors are hiding something at Jericho Castle."

Before anyone could react to Joe and Maxine's accounts, the waiter arrived with a tray laden with drinks: beers for Benjamin, Maxine and Luigi and Cokes for Paul and Joe. Trying to control his increasing agitation, Benjamin drained his glass of beer in one go, slammed the glass on the table and ordered another round of drinks. Rubbing the still-visible and sizeable bump on his head, Benjamin launched into an account of his visit to Jericho Castle.

"That guard is definitely guilty of something and I'm sure he's the miscreant who knocked me out." Benjamin's companions murmured their sympathies, sounding to a bewildered Paul like a hive of angry bees.

"I didn't manage to investigate any parts of the castle properly, but I had my eye on one of the towers flanking a rampart before I was knocked unconscious. I am now convinced that the castle is being used as a hiding place for something valuable and I propose we revisit it, but this time, we need to ensure we do not look suspicious!"

Joe Bertolli shook his head and laughed out loud. "How are YOU going to manage that Benjamin? Your own mother would find you suspicious even when you're sitting at home!"

"Funny man....very funny man. No wonder you never made it beyond sergeant! I am serious Joe. We could go disguised as a group of foreign tourists, or we could co-opt a group of school-kids and act as though we're on a school trip. Maybe we could get Paul's History teacher to organise another trip to the castle and some of us could straggle along disguised as teachers or classroom assistants and..."

Before Benjamin Zeigarnik could complete his zealous ramblings, Paul Kanner interjected with a very rare interruption. "Mr Snow won't go there again!" This was met by belly-laughter from around the table and even Benjamin was amused. The mirth soon turned to feelings of awkwardness and guilt as everyone reflected on Lisa Khan's mishap and Mr Snow's heart-attack.

"So how is Lisa faring Paul?" A very concerned Benjamin Zeigarnik suddenly thought it was time he behaved in a manner in keeping with his station in life. He was aware that his competitive streak would often lead him to making petulant and childish remarks, which he almost always regretted.

Paul looked downcast and distressed. "She's still in rehab. Mr Snow said she'll probably be in a wheelchair for the rest of her life. She's convinced that someone pushed her, but she didn't see anyone."

The sullen atmosphere was broken by Luigi. "As you all now know, I contacted Professor Halva Halloumi to find out what she knows about Jericho Castle. We had a very informative, if short, conversation over the 'phone. She told me something very interesting about the owners of the castle: Old Heritage Holdings. It turns out they are three nefarious characters who knew each other as students. One of them has a criminal record and served time in prison for selling artefacts from the British Museum on the black market. I think these people are mad about money...maybe they are using the castle as a hiding place for valuables, but my guess is they are using the castle to *make* money...and what better way to do this than to increase its notoriety? So I like Benjamin's old idea better than his new one."

The awkward silence that followed Luigi's reflections was broken by Maxine Carter. "Luigi, you mentioned that Professor Halloumi was about to tell you something just before the line went down...what was it?"

"Ah yes! Thank you for reminding me Maxine. When I spoke to her just before I came here Halva told me that on a visit to Jericho Castle she saw a small pile of sand next to the eastern tower at the end of the northern rampart. Very curious!"

The companions looked at one another with varying degrees of puzzlement on their faces. An emboldened Benjamin took up the reins again. "Like I said, we need to investigate Jericho Castle properly!

Having remained quiet for much of the discussion, Paul Kanner decided to try to make sense of the conflicting ideas he'd heard. As if talking to himself, he distilled everything into a few brief points. "If they're hiding stuff at the castle, we need to find what they're hiding. But if they're worried that lots of people are getting close to finding these valuables, why are they continuing to use the castle as a hiding place? Why not just move the stuff someplace else? Surely, their own houses would attract less attention than the castle! But, if they're really just causing accidents to give the place a more exciting reputation, then we need to find evidence that they are causing accidents. The dodgy guard would be useful to them in both scenarios."

Each of the adults around the table became lost in their own thoughts about Jericho Castle. Joe felt it was time to close proceedings. "Thank you Paul for summarising the two possibilities so clearly. You made a very good point regarding the hiding-place idea: why not use a less public place to hide something valuable? Either way, we need to organise another visit to the castle. I need to mull this over and come up with a plan."

Later that night, alone in the comforting gloom of his flat, Joe Bertolli ran his hands over his stubbled chin, sighed and turned on his desktop computer. As it whirred interminably, he smiled at the thought of the adventure on the horizon. When the machine's noise-level descended to a purr, he fired off an e-mail. Tomorrow he and Maxine would be going back to Jericho Castle!

Chapter 11

A Shot in the Dark

Joe Bertolli and Maxine Carter emerged gingerly from their hiding place between the pews of the chapel to begin their investigation.

They had purchased their entry tickets six hours ago in the early afternoon. They arrived looking like a very unremarkable (and unmemorable!) couple. Dressed in dark casual clothes and with an assumed air of bland indifference to their surroundings, they were barely noticed by the other visitors or security staff. Their plan was to search the castle under cover of darkness and away from prying eyes.

The darkness was now almost complete as Joe Bertolli and Maxine Carter tiptoed around the base of one of the watchtowers at Jericho Castle. Having armed themselves with small torches and a burglary

118

kit recovered from the evidence room at Greenwich Police Station, they were about to attempt to find a way into the imposing edifice.

Maxine directed the torch-beam on to a sign on the door: **KEEP OUT. DANGER. VISITORS CANNOT ACCESS THE WATCHTOWERS. STAFF ONLY**. "Joe, this sign is new isn't it? I don't remember seeing it last time we were here."

"You're right. But on our previous visit I did notice an identical sign lying discarded by that wall over there. Very curious!"

Joe turned the spherical brass door handle as he and Maxine leaned against the door with all their weight. The door refused to co-operate and the two detectives realised they would need to resort to unlawful methods of entry. For a drawn-out moment they both retreated into their own private world as the implications of what they were about to do began to percolate through to consciousness. *Imagine the headlines* thought Joe: ***Coppers Charged***

with Breaking and Entering with Burglar's Kit Stolen from Police Station. Maxine's private moment took a very different turn: *would a criminal record prevent her from resuming a career in mathematics once she'd been chucked out of the police force?*

Joe shook the imaginary headline from his head and reached into the kit-bag for a crow-bar. Positioning the crow-bar near the latch Joe attempted to prise the door open, but merely succeeded in setting off a sharp shooting pain in his elbow. Maxine smiled invisibly as she rummaged in the kit-bag. She pulled out a folding-stool and a chisel.

"What do you plan to do with those Maxine, carve your initials while sitting comfortably?"

Maxine snorted, stepped onto the unfolded stool and stretched to reach the arched window located above and to the right of the door. Taking the cutting edge of the chisel to the left-hand edge of the window she began to scrape away at the putty.

The putty was old and brittle and crumbling away quite nicely. Within minutes, Maxine was able to pull out the narrow lancet window and pass it down to Joe. Just as the window was about to exchange hands, they froze in mid-movement. An eerie sound filled the whole bailey behind them.

"What was that?" whispered Joe.

"Sounds like metal being dragged along the ground. Makes me think of dungeons and chains. Do we investigate the source of the sound or carry on here Joe?"

"Let's stick with what we came to do. Can you get through that window-space if I give you a leg-up?" The sound that had set their nerves on edge came to an abrupt end. The sudden silence, like a mid-scene commercial break in an American TV show, left them both disoriented. Maxine took a few seconds to marshal her thoughts before she could reply.

"Yes, I think so...let's try."

121

Joe linked his hands together and steadied himself as Maxine placed first one foot and then the other on his linked palms. "OK Maxine, on the count of three!" As soon as Maxine uttered "three" she found herself being catapulted towards the window. Before she could register even a single thought or feeling, she found herself clasping the empty window-frame. Hauling herself through the gap, she allowed herself to slide hands-first to the ground on the other side, now in the pitch-dark interior of the watchtower.

"Are you OK Maxine?"

"I think so Joe! Let me get my torch on."

"I don't know how I'm going to get in...too big for that small opening. Could you try the door from the inside Maxine?"

Maxine's efforts to open the door from the inside went unrewarded. She would have to snoop around the watchtower on her own.

"Maxine, I'm going to snoop around out here

and see if I can find out what caused that eerie sound. Let's rendezvous in fifteen minutes at 20.35."

Turning around, Maxine shone her torch around the space in the near-distance and could see the spiral stone staircase that she had been expecting. She approached the first step and as she began to ascend the steps began to feel gripped by vertigo. The balancing mechanisms of her inner ear and brain were disconcerted by the fact that her eyes could not see the spiral path that her feet were trying to follow. The torch produced only a narrow beam of light which made it almost impossible to anticipate the next step.

~~~~~~~~~~

Joe Bertolli tip-toed towards the barbican, his heart racing and his upper lip moist with sweat. He guessed that the sound had come from the barbican. As he approached, he turned on his torch, squinted his eyes and proceeded to survey the area in front of him. He felt anxious and exposed as the torch-beam would be visible to any nefarious character who might be skulking around. As he edged right up to the portcullis he noticed it wasn't fully lowered and had a gap of several inches from the ground.

Bending to inspect the lower part of the portcullis, Joe was startled by a sudden sound in the distance behind him. It sounded like someone shuffling along the ground in carpet slippers, a gentle sound that was as loud and frightening as a pistol-shot in the quiet night of the castle bailey. He decided to leave his inspection of the portcullis and barbican for another time and headed back toward the sound.

~~~~~~~~~~

Maxine was making steady progress in her ascent of the spiral staircase. Now that her eyes had adjusted to the dark, she could see a small landing a few steps ahead. Reaching the landing, she shone her torch at the wall, looking for any signs of a doorway into a room. The wall was uniform and seemed like a normal, solid castle wall. *Why is there a landing here then? And surely, the tower is much wider than the stairway? There must be rooms somewhere in here.* Maxine extended the palms of both hands and touching the wall, made a circular motion like that of car windscreen wipers. She wondered whether part of the wall served as a concealed entrance and hoped that she might discern any irregularities in the wall.

Some minutes later, Maxine snagged her right-hand little finger as her hands swept the wall in a right-ward direction. There was a ridged edge in the stonework here...*could it be a disguised door?* She tried to grip the ridge with all her fingers in an attempt to prise open the potential door, but could not achieve a good enough grip. *If only she had access to the tools that she'd left outside in the burglar-bag!* She quickly shone the torch on her watchface: **20:32**...*almost time to meet Joe.* She could meet him, tell him about her discovery and return with some suitable tools. *It was going to be a long night. Thank goodness that it was Sunday tomorrow!*

As Maxine began her slow descent of the spiral staircase, she could hear a rattling sound coming from the entrance door down below. *Must be Joe trying to signal to me that it's time to rendezvous.*

No sooner had she completed that thought than she could hear a distinct click and the sound of the door creaking open. It didn't take anyone of Maxine's high level of intelligence to realise that whoever was at the door was *not* Joe. Maxine turned off the torchlight and groped her way quietly back up the staircase. She realised that unless the intruder had left the door unlocked, she'd be trapped in here and at his mercy. Feeling a reassuring draft of cool air that was a sure sign that the door had been left open, she continued her ascent to a point just beyond the landing she'd encountered earlier. She sat on a step in silence waiting in the hope that the intruder headed directly for the hidden doorway that she thought she'd discovered.

The intruder's ascent was painfully slow and ungainly. Maxine was beginning to wonder whether he was none other than the moustachioed security guard who raised their suspicions on their previous visit...he had a limp! The tension she felt was momentarily broken by a series of sounds emanating from outside. Before she could identify the sounds she found herself being yanked by invisible hands and felt herself tumbling down the bruising steps.

Bruised and disoriented, Maxine felt a heavy weight on her ankle. She couldn't locate her torch, which she realised must have fallen from her grasp when she fell. She eventually managed to summon the energy to bend from her waist toward the dead weight pinning down her foot. Stretching her right arm as far as it would go, she made contact with a rough and stubbly surface. She recoiled in horror at the dawning realisation that the object weighing down her foot was a body. As she began to regain her senses, the body in question emitted a long low groan.

"Uhhhhhhhhhhhhhhh...damn...my head." It was the unmistakable voice of Sgt Joe Bertolli.

"Joe! What happened?"

"Uhhh...that's my question Maxine. What happened to you?"

Initially competing to have the other's story heard first, the two colleagues eventually managed to communicate the essential details of what had befallen them. Joe recounted how he had more-or-less stumbled on Maxine's prostrate body. Almost as soon as he had seen Maxine's expressionless face in his torch-beam he was enveloped in darkness again.

Gingerly rubbing the crown of his head, Joe

continued with his story. "I came back here from investigating the portcullis at the barbican because I was convinced that some miscreant had scurried in this direction. The tower door was slightly ajar, and I realised he must have entered the tower. He must have been hiding someplace on the stairway landing and coshed me when I bent over to help you."

"We both said that the assailant seemed to be ungainly in his movement and...well, I wondered whether he's the creepy security guard that we saw last time we were here."

"The same thought had occurred to me!" Joe shone his torch on his watch. "How time flies! It's already 22.23. I suspect our friend won't come back any time soon, now that we're together and both conscious."

"Yes, what a formidable pair we make!"

"Shall we continue with our snooping PC Carter?"

"Are you asking me to engage in unlawful

activities *sir*?"

"We *are* the law PC Carter! Now tell me, where did you get to before you were so rudely interrupted?"

Retrieving a flat-headed screwdriver from the kit-bag outside, Maxine returned to the landing with Joe in her wake. With Joe acting as torch-bearer, Maxine inserted the tip of the screwdriver and gently tried to lever the ridge towards her. They heard a low creaking sound, followed by a gentle susurration of falling sand. The wall ridge now protruded outwards by an inch. Stretching and repeating the process higher up the wall, Maxine was able to force the ridge out by a further two inches. She and Joe each grasped the exposed edge with their fingertips and pulled in unison with all their strength. The wall came away with a loud scraping noise and revealed itself to be a concealed door, as Maxine had suspected.

His torch-beam beginning to falter and on the

blink, Joe Bertolli crept into the cold space, only to be met by another blow to the head...this time, it was his forehead bumping into a pull-cord. He yanked on the cord and the space came to life in localised pools of studio lights. Maxine Carter followed him in the room, her jaw hanging in disbelief. The room was crammed from floor to ceiling with a vast array of tools and gadgets, including long barge-poles and grappling-hooks. This was someone's arsenal-cum-workshop!

"I think we've seen enough Maxine. This hideaway has all the equipment anyone would ever need to wreak havoc and devastation in this place."

Chapter 12

Every Picture Tells a Story

Mr Kanner's fist froze just as it was about to make contact with Paul's bedroom door. He was stopped in his tracks by a curious sound emanating from within. Paul was known to produce sounds of protest on most school-day mornings, especially on Mondays, but this was an altogether different sound...and on a Sunday morning too! After a few seconds, the sound ceased and Mr Kanner turned the door-handle and entered Paul's room. He was assailed by a terrifying sight! Paul was dressed in full football kit and was making fresh sounds that Mr Kanner now realised were in mimicry of combative sportsmen..."Go on then, on my head...over here...pass it pass it!"

On seeing his dad gawping in his direction, Paul

132

came to his senses with a jolt. "Erm...hi dad... er... practising... um."

Mr Kanner scanned Paul's room and noticed that Paul's laptop was showing a football-practice session involving the local English Football League team, Charlton Athletic. Players were arrayed in red shirts, while some were further adorned by fluorescent yellow bibs. Mr Kanner smiled inwardly at the uncharitable thought that fleeted briefly through his mind: Paul's room had never seen so much action before.

"So Paul, tell me, *what* exactly is it that you're practising?"

"Er...football! Have a five-a-side match in the playground tomorrow lunchtime."

"Excellent Paul. So pleased that you're getting into some social stuff. You certainly *sounded* the part of a footballer just then! Anyway, I came up here to ask whether you'd heard any more about your injured classmate Lisa. We were just talking to the

133

neighbours about it over the garden fence and I realised that we hadn't heard anything new in a couple of weeks."

"Er...nothing new dad. Still in rehab..."

"OK Paul, see you downstairs in a bit. Breakfast in half an hour."

Paul was suddenly overwhelmed by everything. Learning how to do football talk was quite taxing, but thinking about Lisa's tragedy was unbearable. He tried to think of the mishap as one element of a complicated pattern that had to be solved to save lives and ensure kids' wellbeing.

In his less guarded moments, Paul tended to imagine the child victims of whatever was going on at Jericho Castle. *But it wasn't just kids!* Paul was particularly intrigued by the case of the missing historian...Dr Marcus Beard. *How can an adult go missing for five years? Surely, he must have been killed and buried someplace...*

Leaning across the keyboard, he exited the

football-practice video and googled the missing historian's name: 'Dr Marcus Beard'. Various familiar newspaper articles appeared, but on this occasion Paul focused on a less familiar image of the unfortunate historian. A youthful Dr Beard was shown in his book-strewn office at the University of Kent. Paul's attention was drawn to a wall in the picture that was adorned by what appeared to be a framed picture of some kind of coat of arms. Could this be the coat of arms of the university? Paul googled 'coat of arms University of Kent' and saw a very different image, containing castle buildings, two lions, three blackbirds and a white horse. The picture on Dr Beard's wall showed a shield with three red eagles (or were they griffins?) each adorned with a golden crown.

Googling various combinations of descriptive keywords including **coat of arms three red eagles griffins golden crowns**, Paul came across a number of similar designs, but none quite like the one that

135

appeared in the picture before him. Paul wondered whether his History teacher Mr Snow might be able to help him track this down. Paul downloaded and saved the picture and was just about to log off when his e-mail alert pinged: it was a message from Joe Bertolli.

Joe's e-mail was also copied to Maxine, Benjamin and Luigi. In it, Joe had recounted details of the previous night's escapades with Maxine at Jericho Castle. Joe's e-mail transported Paul to some inner recess of his mind as he tried to make sense of everything they had uncovered so far about the Jericho Castle incidents. His dad's echoing voice from downstairs barely registered in his thoughts.

Chapter 13

Heraldic Devices

It was Monday morning, 07.48 according to the clock in the detectives' open-plan office. Detective Police Constable Maxine Carter was struggling to keep awake and she feared she had a long day ahead of her. The traumatising experiences at Jericho Castle kept her awake most of last night and Saturday night and her brain felt like mush.

She promised DCI Gravesham that she'd make some inroads into a new case today; a bank robbery with some distinctive and unusual features. She needed to consult the National Crime Data-Base, but dreaded the thought of embarking on what she would normally consider to be an interesting puzzle. *It was going to be a very long day.*

As she opened her browser, she found several

e-mail alerts waiting for her, including one from Joe Bertolli and one from Paul Kanner. *Ugh! More Jericho Castle stuff no doubt. I'll look at it later...much later!* Her hands and eyes seemed unaware of her thoughts as both e-mails were opened and read in the ensuing seconds.

Maxine's aversion to all things connected to Jericho Castle evaporated as soon as her eyes focused on the picture that Paul had sent. Maxine stared at the man's face for some seconds as she sought to recollect where she had seen him before. *He looked familiar...well, vaguely familiar. I probably saw something like this before when Paul was showing us stuff about the missing historian.* She then glanced at the coat of arms on the historian's office wall. Paul had asked her to help him find out the family to whom this belonged. Maxine knew of a woman who was an expert on heraldry and she made a mental note to look up her contact details later and seek her help. For now, she needed strong black coffee and plenty of it.

After her second revitalising mug of coffee, Maxine closed her eyes while pretending to be looking at her computer screen. There were three other detectives in the room, including Joe Bertolli, who seemed to be in a trance in the far corner of the room. Closing her eyes even for a minute always seemed to lift the fog from her overwrought mind. Feeling calmer and less weary than she had twenty minutes before, Maxine allowed her mind to return to the mysteriously missing Dr Marcus Beard and his coat of arms.

She googled **Beard coat of arms** and found several heraldic designs, but none even remotely matching the one on Dr Beard's wall. On a whim, she decided to see what she could find out about Dr Beard's family tree. Entering the few details she had into an ancestry website, she came across several entries for people with the name **Marcus Beard**. Only three of these related to people who had the same

139

year of birth as the missing historian. The second entry caught her eye: **Marcus Beard: Father = Gregor Beard; Mother = Danielle de Courcy.** *Bingo! Marcus Beard's mother was a de Courcy, and possibly related to Guy de Courcy, founder of Jericho Castle!*

Barely able to contain her excitement, Maxine googled one last search-term: **de Courcy coat of arms.** It matched! The image before her was identical to the one in the picture that Paul Kanner had sent. Taking a screen-shot of the de Courcy coat of arms, she fired off an e-mail to Paul Kanner and went to revive the sagging Joe Bertolli.

"Joe! I think we're onto something here. The missing historian, Marcus Beard, is a descendant of the guy who built Jericho Castle."

A dazed Joe Bertolli could barely keep upright in his chair as he gazed uncomprehendingly at Maxine. "Sorry...what did you say?"

"Paul alerted me to a picture of the coat of arms on Marcus Beard's office wall...you know, the missing historian?"

"OK...and?"

"It turns out that the coat of arms belongs to the de Courcy family. As you'll doubtless remember, Guy de Courcy was the founder of Jericho Castle. I've done some research into Marcus Beard's family tree and it turns out his mother is a de Courcy!"

As Maxine's revelations began to penetrate the mist of his befuddled brain, a wry smile formed on Joe Bertolli's lips. "I think we need to get pally with Old Heritage Holdings. We need to find a pretext for interviewing them. Marcus Beard must have posed a threat to them...maybe he knew something that they

wanted kept hidden!"

Chapter 14

Hidden Motives

Paul Kanner lay in the centre of the football pitch, his nose gushing copious quantities of blood. As he looked in the near-distance, he could see the sniggering face of Boris Jackson, one of John Cameron's minions. In his slightly stunned state he slowly realised that the sharp object that he'd felt in his face a few minutes ago was the knobbly elbow of Jackson.

"Hold your head up Mr Kanner! We need to staunch that bleeding of yours. Mr Angelopoulos, if you'd be good enough to run along to my office *post haste* and fetch the first aid kit...it's on the floor under my desk." Mr Patrick Boateng, head of Physical Education looked benignly at Paul, as he knelt down to examine the extent of his injuries.

"You'll live Mr Kanner...but I bet it'll be a bit painful once the shock has worn off. Ah, Mr Angelopoulos, thank you." As Mr Boateng gently applied a sterile dressing to Paul's nose, he surreptitiously looked at the kit-clad group who were beginning to drift away. Most of the kids' faces were frowning with concern, but one boy stood out from the rest: Boris Jackson, whose wry smile suggested something was definitely amiss. *It wouldn't be the first time that the oafish clown had intentionally hurt a fellow-student.*

"Mr Angelopoulos, would you kindly escort Mr Kanner to the nurse's station please? It would be a great kindness if you spent the remaining twenty minutes of the games period with Mr Kanner."

As Paul Kanner was slowly led away by Demis Angelopoulos, Mr Boateng started to hatch a plan of re-education: *Boris Jackson will be appointed to the role of class first aid monitor. He will have to attend to injured players and escort them to the nurse where necessary. Will he see it as a promotion or as a punishment? Either way, it will be in his best interests to rein-in his excessive "competitiveness" during games.*

While the nurse tended to his injury, Paul began to reflect in a more focused way on what had just taken place on the football pitch. It seemed to him that his arch-nemesis John Cameron had eased off in his persecution of him, but the slack seemed to have been taken up by his cronies. *Why were Cameron's friends getting worse while Cameron himself was becoming less sarcastic and oafish?*

Tiring of the imponderable oddities of his peers' behaviour, Paul turned his attention to Jericho Castle. He hadn't heard anything from Joe Bertolli for a while. *Maybe nothing new has been discovered.*

~~~~~~~~~~

Sgt Joe Bertolli lifted the smoking bonnet of his

Ford Capri and immediately slammed it shut. "You're a bloody heap of rubbish! You will be replaced by a new model! I hate you! You've really let me down this time!"

The Capri had chosen a particularly inconvenient place to break down. Joe had just got on to Tower Bridge when his car produced an almighty explosion and had then ground to a spluttering halt. Tower Bridge connected south London to central and north London over the River Thames. The bridge always posed a challenging route for motorists as it was a drawbridge that had to cater to river traffic as well as road traffic. The usual delays were made even worse for the motorists behind Bertolli's car. In the midst of aggressive honking from neighbouring vehicles, Bertolli attempted to communicate with the AA Recovery Service on his mobile phone. He stewed in anger and embarrassment as the life-long minutes passed very slowly. At last, like a mirage, a yellow recovery vehicle appeared. The Ford Capri was unceremoniously put on tow while a shame-faced Joe Bertolli jumped into the cabin's passenger seat. He smiled wanly at the driver and uttered his sheepish thanks before taking out his mobile to warn Benjamin Zeigarnik that he'd be late.

Dr Benjamin Zeigarnik was seated at a window table in *Le Pont de la Tour*, his favourite French restaurant in London. Drinking his third cup of black coffee, he looked at his watch and shook his head; *Joe was late again*. Joe had called him more than ten minutes ago to explain why he was running late, but Benjamin was very hungry and was losing patience. *Tower Bridge is only a five-minute walk from here...has he lost his way?* While Benjamin was cursing inwardly, Sgt Joe Bertolli made a sudden and dramatic appearance, first walking into the glass door before tripping over the outstretched leg of a customer.

"At last! The knight of the realm has come to

grace us after losing his trusty white steed! Sit Sir Joe and let us order straight away...I'm famished! I'm not used to eating my lunch over an hour later than my stomach expects it!"

"Sorry Benjamin. I must do something about that wretched car."

"Yes, why not send it for burial?"

"You're such an empathic psychologist Benjamin! Remind me to come to you when I have troubles. Anyway, it's good for you to skip a meal or two...you're not exactly wasting away."

The two friends took a cursory look at the menus. Benjamin ordered *escargot* in garlic-butter sauce followed by *coq au vin*. Joe settled for a *boeuf bourguignon.*

Joe pulled out his mobile and showed Benjamin the picture of Dr Marcus Beard that Paul Kanner had sent to Maxine Carter. He explained that Marcus Beard was a descendant of Guy de Courcy, the founder of Jericho Castle.

"He looks a little bit familiar. I think his picture reminds me of the portrait of Guy de Courcy in the castle. Hm...so did the missing historian stand to inherit the castle at some point?"

"I don't know Benjamin. Maxine has done a little digging and discovered that Beard's maternal grandfather sold the castle in the 1980s to an American businessman. It turns out that Guy de Courcy specified in his will that if anyone who inherits the place cannot afford to maintain the structure to a high standard, then it should be sold to someone outside the family who has the requisite financial resources. Beard's grandfather was broke, having lost a lot of money in a business venture that went wrong. It turns out that the American who bought it, Don Trumpington, was happy to restore the castle to its former glory. Unfortunately, he was not interested in continuing de Courcy's original legacy and used the castle as an investment. After Trumpington restored the castle, he placed it in virtual cold storage and just rented out a few of the rooms to wealthy tourists. When Trumpington died, it was inherited by his playboy son Don Jr., who neglected the place for many years. It was eventually sold to Old Heritage Holdings about eight years ago."

Benjamin Zeigarnik's response was forestalled by the arrival of his starter. He wolfed down the *escargot* and drained half a bottle of mineral water before he spoke. "So Old Heritage Holdings have restored the castle and continued de Courcy's legacy of educating today's youth in castle lore. But why? What do they stand to gain from this?"

"The castle definitely has some dodgy deal connected to it. Look what happened to you when you went snooping around the place. Look what happened to Maxine and me when we last went there! That security man with the moustache and the over-developed curiosity is obviously being paid to be suspicious of visitors and I would bet that he's the one who attacked us."

"OK Joe, I'm with you so far. So, the new people bought the castle because they thought it housed some kind of hidden valuables, like in the rumours we've heard about. But why did Marcus Beard disappear from the castle a few years ago? Did he find something and decided to go into hiding?"

"Or maybe he was kidnapped Benjamin. Maybe he knew something. Maybe he contacted Old Heritage Holdings and threatened to expose some secrets. Perhaps he had been blackmailing them for a while and they decided it was time to put this little problem to bed."

Benjamin Zeigarnik's nose twitched visibly at the wafted aromas of the approaching *Coq au vin* and *boeuf bourguignon*.

"Bon appetite Messieurs!"

The two friends barely looked at each other as they devoured their sumptuous meals and all thoughts of Jericho Castle disappeared into the ether.

"Well my friend, it looks as though neither of us is driving today. How about a little *cognac* or two to aid the digestion?"

Joe responded to Benjamin's rhetorical question with a smile as Benjamin summoned the waiter. Within seconds, the two men were staring at the bottle of *Hennessy cognac* that stood guard between the pair of bowl-shaped brandy glasses. Perhaps they had eaten too much too quickly...both men struggled to take command of their thoughts. Their arms were in synchrony as each reached out for his drink.

The spell was broken by Joe. "We need to find a pretext for interviewing the owners of Old Heritage Holdings. What did Luigi say he'd learned from Professor Halloumi? The three owners knew each other from their student days well before they formed the company and bought Jericho Castle. Apparently, each of them had been accused of committing a crime."

Joe Bertolli and Benjamin Zeigarnik slowly retreated into their own private worlds as the soothing effects of the *cognac* began to take hold.

Chapter 15

Old Heritage Holdings in the News

Sgt Joe Bertolli was seated at his desk suppressing wave after wave of yawns. Maxine Carter had agreed to give him lifts into work for the rest of the week until his Ford Capri had been fixed. Maxine's Citroén C4 was a trustier and speedier car and got them to Greenwich Police Station ten minutes earlier than planned.

By the time he'd drained his second polystyrene cup of black coffee, Joe was on the verge of hatching a plan. He and Benjamin had agreed yesterday that the next stage into the investigation of Jericho Castle was to try to wrestle information from the new owners, Old Heritage Holdings. Joe was growing more suspicious of the three criminal-types who owned the castle: Julia Perkins, a former dodgy employee of the British Museum; Patrick

Leyton, bent banker; and Victoria Singh, corrupt archaeologist. One difficulty was that as a member of the Metropolitan Police, he had no jurisdiction over possible crimes committed in Hertfordshire. His earlier enquiries revealed that Hertfordshire Police had come up with nothing in their own investigations and had closed the case file. He further reflected that Maxine had been right from the beginning: this would have to be a private investigation to the very end, at which point they would have solved the case or been sacked...or possibly both!

Joe Bertolli realised that he would have to resort to the dark arts of subterfuge in order to get anywhere near to extracting information from the Old Heritage Holdings crew. He had a fleeting and vague thought that the young Paul Kanner could play a vital part in this venture, though precisely what form this would take was eluding him for now. With legs outstretched and eyes closed, Joe started to drift off into a gentle reverie.

"Joe!" PC Maxine Carter strode with urgency and excitement to Joe's desk. "Wake up! I've found out something!"

Joe stretched his arms, yawned and blinked. "Ah...Maxine...what did you say?"

"I've conducted some internet searches and I've found out something important! The three owners of Jericho Castle have been washing their dirty laundry in all the business newspapers. It turns out there have been some major rifts in the last couple of years. Julia Perkins has been battling against Patrick Leyton and Victoria Singh in a war of attrition. She claims her two co-owners have colluded in a dirty-tricks campaign to oust her from Old Heritage Holdings. One article in the *Financial Times* gave a lengthy account of a social media blitz discrediting Perkins and claiming that her share of the investment in Jericho Castle came from ill-gotten gains when she'd worked at the British Museum. Hertfordshire Police have just opened up a new investigation."

Joe Bertolli gazed through the farside window into the distance while the cobwebbed gears of his brain tried to crank out a response to Maxine's revelations. "That's brilliant Maxine! Maybe we could tempt her into unwittingly revealing some secrets about the castle. If we pose as reporters interested in *her side* of the story, she might cough up something useful to our investigations, such as..."

"Hold on Joe! I am not getting involved in anything as underhand and criminal as what you're proposing. It would be career suicide for sure and maybe even a spell in prison! We have to be both above-board and clever about this."

Joe Bertolli smiled weakly as he realised that he'd allowed himself to be carried away by his enthusiasm for solving the case. He nodded his head in acknowledgement of Maxine's words of wisdom and began to massage his forehead, willing calmer and more sensible ideas to come to the fore. "OK.

You're right of course. We need to think of an alternative. Any ideas?"

Maxine Carter stroked her chin while staring at the ground, willing her brain to come up with ideas. She shook her head, let out a sigh and opened her palms to the sky in defeat. "No ideas Joe. I have no ideas at all. Maybe we need to convene another brainstorming session with young Paul, Benjamin and Luigi."

~~~~~~~~~~

It was Saturday lunchtime and Nelson Road was buzzing with university students and tourists taking advantage of the unseasonably good weather. Joe Bertolli had arranged to meet the others at the cafeteria of the National Maritime Museum in Greenwich, which was a short walk from Paul Kanner's house. He parked his repaired and rejuvenated Ford Capri in the museum car-park and made his way along the crunching footpath to the main entrance of the museum. As he ascended the stairs leading to the cafeteria he heard a loud guffaw. This unmistakable trade-mark of Dr Benjamin Zeigarnik brought a smile to Joe's face as he stepped onto the cafeteria floor.

The loud voice and laughter of Benjamin Zeigarnik dominated the cafeteria as Joe Bertolli approached the table where his friends were seated. "The detective is here! Hello Joe my friend! Good of you to join us. I had almost forgotten that you were the one who arranged this happy gathering." Joe grimaced at Benjamin in reply and smiled wanly at his seated friends.

Joe seated himself in the remaining seat between Paul Kanner and Maxine Carter, tickled at the thought that Paul might have kept this seat especially for him. "Good to see you Paul. Er...do you visit this place much?"

Paul gazed at Joe's ear and nodded in the

affirmative. "I come here mainly to see the stuff on Shackleton's Antarctic expeditions. I've been coming here since I was six years old. Er...I've been allowed to come here on my own since I was twelve years of age. My mum and dad they...find it boring." Paul's growing confidence was evident for all to see. Joe smiled as he conceded to himself that Benjamin Zeigarnik was a force for good, even though he could be a royal pain.

Once everyone had settled down with coffees and cokes, Joe leaned into the table conspiratorially, his action being reciprocated by the other group members. After summarising Maxine Carter's revelations concerning the schism among the owners of Old Heritage Holdings, Joe set them to work on his problem: "OK...in a nutshell, I'd like to hear any ideas you might have for extracting information from Julia Perkins that don't involve breaking the law."

The deafening silence that followed was broken by the stentorian voice of Benjamin

Zeigarnik. "Ahem! Well, I have an idea that might just work. In my capacity as a psychologist I can request an interview on the basis that her story would be of interest to me. I too am bound by ethical constraints and will not be able to lie to her. But I can legitimise the interview by offering to write a piece on competitiveness in the relationships of friends who become colleagues. I could then, with her permission, make legitimate use of her interview transcript and you would be able to use anything that comes out in the interview."

Benjamin's suggestion was met with a collection of knitted brows and other expressions of puzzlement. Joe was more sympathetic to Benjamin's idea than the others, but needed reassurance. "Benjamin, let me make sure I understand you correctly. You contact Julia Perkins and tell her that you are a psychologist who is doing research on friends who become colleagues and you wish to interview her. Presumably, you'd need to explain why you've chosen her as one of your interviewees. Presumably, you'll also refer to the problems in her relationships with Patrick Leyton and Victoria Singh that were covered in the business newspapers. You would then write an actual article that would include material from the interview and attempt to get this published in a journal or magazine of some kind?" Benjamin's nodding head signalled that Joe had understood his proposal. "OK, so how will you manage to probe her on issues that are relevant to our investigation? Surely, you'll have to focus all your questions on changes in her relationships with the other two. It seems to me extremely unlikely that she will divulge any secrets in such a controlled context. And anyway, what's in it for her? Why would she agree to such an interview?"

"Maybe if Benjamin's article says good things about what she's done at Jericho Castle she'd be happy. Maybe this would make her want to be interviewed?" Paul's soft voice had everyone straining to hear.

Maxine nodded encouragingly at Paul who by this time had his eyes firmly fastened to the parquet flooring beneath the table. "Good idea Paul! We need to focus on what would motivate her to talk. The promise of an article that puts her in a good light might entice her. But if she knows any secrets, I don't see how she could be tricked into letting these slip."

Benjamin's agitation grew as he felt his influence wane. "We need to find a topic that she's passionate about. Passions loosen people's tongues in my experience."

Luigi Pecorino spoke for the first time. "What do we know about this Julia Perkins? Professor Halloumi tells me that she studied history at university but was also motivated by prestige and money. Maybe these are her passions. Between them, Benjamin and Paul may well be right: interview her about her successes and the people who are trying to do her down. But add the other

163

ingredient: her interest...or passion?...for history. Maybe she'll tell us about how her love of history got her involved in the prestigious role of a co-owner of Jericho Castle. Who knows, maybe provoking her by suggesting that Jericho Castle is not *real history* might agitate her into letting something slip about something real in the castle."

Luigi's remarks were met by a collective stunned silence. It was beginning to dawn on everyone that this was going to be a very intricate operation.

Benjamin, now in a less cavalier mood responded in a sombre voice "Luigi, your analysis is very incisive...you should have become a psychologist! We need to think of a pretext for the interview so that we can capture all the passions you mention. It looks as though we'll need a very high-profile and skilled interviewer who is associated with a well-known magazine to pull this off. We will also need to structure the interview very tightly, like a play-script, to maximise our chances of getting her to slip up and divulge a secret or two."

Crestfallen, Joe Bertolli rubbed his ears vigorously, as though attempting to erase what he was hearing. "Er...I now think this approach is not going to work. I can't see Julia Perkins divulging anything significant about Old Heritage Holdings or Jericho Castle. She'd have little to gain and potentially much to lose. We need to take a different tack."

Joe's statement left a pall of gloom in the assembled group as the hopelessness of the situation sank into the deepest depths of everyone's mind. Everyone was very still with eyes rooted to the floor. Paul Kanner was the first to rouse himself from the collective malaise. He became quite agitated and opened his mouth to speak but then checked himself. He began to stretch and then flex each of his fingers in an attempt to soothe his nerves and marshal his thoughts. Finally, he uttered a word.

"Kids!" Everyone abruptly tore their gaze from the floor and looked up expectantly at Paul's face.

"Erm...kids like stories. Stories about secrets...and...er... treasure. If Julia Perkins thinks it's for kids she might try to make it more exciting by mentioning something new about Jericho Castle. She won't be worried about getting into trouble with a child readership." Paul's elaboration on his initial monosyllabic declamation left everyone stunned.

Joe Bertolli gazed at Paul with a mixture of admiration and concern. "I like your idea Paul, but how can we get this off the ground?"

Paul's look of puzzlement seemed to act as a direct cue to Luigi Pecorino, who had until this point being mulling over various proposals of his own. "One of my most brilliant old history students works as a writer for the kids' magazine, *History Revealed*. I think the promise of a good meal at *Café Roma* and a good bottle of wine should entice her to agree to interview Julia Perkins. She could approach her on the pretext that she's writing a piece on Jericho Castle."

Joe Bertolli's sense of dejection evaporated upon hearing Luigi's idea. "That sounds great Luigi! You do have some surprises up your sleeve! Do you think we'll need to be forthright with your former student about our objectives?"

"Not entirely. Leave it with me my friend."

Chapter 16

To Old Heritage Holdings HQ

It was the last school period on Friday afternoon and Paul Kanner found himself slipping ever deeper into a daydream. He usually enjoyed the Physics class, but his mind was elsewhere today. His excitement had grown since the previous weekend when Joe Bertolli and Luigi Pecorino had invited him to take part in interviewing Julia Perkins, one of the owners of Jericho Castle. He would be working alongside Adebi Adewumi, a writer for *History Revealed*. Joe was particularly proud of the fact that his name would be printed alongside Adebi's byline in the magazine.

"Kanner! Where are you?"

Paul shook himself as he peered in the general direction of Mr Tallis. "I'm here sir!"

"You could have fooled me Kanner! I don't suppose you can tell me anything about today's lesson, can you?" Jeers and laughter erupted throughout the classroom. Paul was gradually learning to discount his peers' frequent eruptions. He willed himself to stay calm as he scratched around for a feasible answer.

"Yes sir, I can. It's about the electromagnetic spectrum."

"Well don't let me catch you drifting off again then!"

Paul was very perplexed by the seemingly illogical statements that his teachers made from time-to-time, but realised that he'd probably got off lightly today...Mr Tallis must be in a good mood.

Just as the lesson was drawing to a close, Paul felt a violent poke in his back. As he turned, he was blinded by a searing light followed by the visual after-effect of a cascade of exploding colours. It was none other than John Cameron. "Just in case you missed the practical demo on the electromagnetic spectrum!" Paul gazed dismissively at Cameron's torch and smiled wryly. "Nice one John!"

<center>~~~~~~~~~~</center>

It had been a very long day at work but she forced herself to check her private e-mail account as soon as she had arrived home at her riverside flat in Greenwich Peninsula. There it was: the e-mail she'd been expecting from her old university tutor, Dr Luigi Pecorino. Adebi Adewumi clicked and downloaded the Word file in the attachment, which contained the interview schedule.

Adebi reflected with nostalgia on her university days when she'd studied history. She smiled warmly as she recalled Luigi's gentle words of encouragement when as an unconfident immigrant youngster she had felt at times that it was all too much for her. Luigi even went so far as to declare her a "genius" at the end of her first year, but Adebi had taken that with a pinch of salt. She felt eternally in his debt, not least for writing a glowing reference when she applied to the BBC for the traineeship on the *History Revealed* magazine. Luigi had urged her to continue on to a Masters degree, but at the time, she had been desperate to earn some money and to popularise history for a new generation of young people.

She knitted her brows in puzzlement as she quickly scanned the interview questions contained in Luigi's document. Some of the questions looked very different from the ones that she routinely asked on the innumerable interviews she had conducted for the magazine. Several of the questions were written in red...these were to be asked by the young man who would be accompanying her, Paul Kanner. Luigi explained that there was a "higher purpose" to the interview, but she was left in the dark about the specific aim of all this. It was going to be a tough interview to conduct, but at least Julia Perkins had readily agreed to the interview, telling her that as a history graduate herself, she was more than happy to appear in a magazine aimed at budding historians.

Adebi printed two copies of the interview schedule and placed them in her work-bag. She had a vague sense of trepidation as she planned tomorrow's route to Jericho Castle.

~~~~~~~~~~

Fighting the urge to sleep, Julia Perkins flicked open the cover of the latest issue of *History Revealed*, which featured articles on the Black Death and life in the plague years. She closed her eyes and cast her mind back to her years as a history student. For a while, she had been quite committed to the idea of pursuing a career as a professional historian and often daydreamed of working for a magazine such as this. Those were heady, idealistic days when anything was possible, so long as it was far enough into the future. *What had happened to those dreams? They were ruined when she met Patrick Leyton and Victoria Singh! Her life had been overshadowed by her love-hate relationship with these two "friends" ever since. They were the ones who'd coerced her into illegal activity when she worked at the British Museum and now they were accusing her of all sorts of things so as to take over her share of Old Heritage Holdings.*

She flicked through the remaining pages of the magazine, her eyes settling on the penultimate page, which advertised future editions of the magazine. There it was: in two months' time, the special edition on Castles: Medieval and Modern. Her interview with Adebi Adewumi will appear there. This would be her opportunity to vindicate herself. She could explain how much she loved history; and indeed, was the only one of the three owners who had this passion

173

and who had educational aspirations for Jericho Castle. Maybe she could drop a secret or two into the conversation: Leyton and Singh could complain all they liked.

Julia Perkins tossed the magazine on to the coffee table and opened the Notes app on her 'phone. *It's time to plan for tomorrow's interview.* She guessed that being interviewed by a very bright reporter and a very bright teenager was going to be very challenging. She needed to anticipate their questions and be clear in her own mind as to how much she was willing to divulge.

<center>~~~~~~~~~~</center>

It was Saturday morning and a barking Bella was hot on Paul's heels as he ran down the stairs to answer the door. Joe Bertolli had arrived to drive Paul to Jericho Castle, where he would meet Adebi Adewumi from *History Revealed* an hour before they were due to interview Julia Perkins. If anyone asked, Joe was Paul's dad, his chauffeur for the day.

Parking the Ford Capri on a side road near the castle, Joe spotted Adebi's smart Peugeot 208 on the other side of the road. Motioning to Paul, they both strode across and introduced themselves.

Adebi led the way to a nearby café where the three conspirators would spend the next forty-five minutes or so. Joe noticed that Paul appeared a little more relaxed than usual and attributed this to Adebi's pleasant manner. Adebi looked towards Paul without making the usual mistake that people made of gazing into his eyes. In a soft voice, she sought to win his confidence and find out a little about him. "So Paul...I gather that you'll be asking Ms Perkins a few questions as well?"

"Um...yes. I have four questions to ask." Paul smiled with a sense of pride that he would be working alongside this renowned reporter.

"Did you come up with these questions

175

yourself Paul?"

"Yes I did. Erm...I suggested them in my meeting with Joe, Benjamin and Luigi. They said they were good questions."

Adebi's eyes widened at the thought that this diminutive fourteen-year-old had dreamt up such incisive questions. "So Paul, you know my old teacher, Luigi Pecorino?"

"Yes. He's a very nice man and a brilliant chef. He's...er...very kind."

"You and I are definitely on the same side Paul. Luigi is a lovely human being and a great teacher."

Paul looked slightly puzzled for an instant and Adebi was worried that she had lost the connection she had been making with him. She decided to refocus on the interview schedule. "I don't know about you Paul, but I am very excited about meeting this Ms Julia Perkins. From what I've read about her, she seems an intriguing and perplexing character."

Paul looked thoughtful. Adebi Adewumi

glanced at Joe Bertolli quizzically. "So, Sgt Bertolli, I hope we'll get some answers that will help you in your investigation. Luigi was uncharacteristically coy when I asked him to explain the true purpose of this interview with Julia Perkins. If I didn't trust Luigi so completely I'd be having some serious scruples right now."

"Please call me Joe Ms...Adebi. I'm sorry about the cloak-and-dagger secrecy, but we'd like you to be as natural as possible when interviewing Julia Perkins. A lot rides on this interview, but we'd like you to treat this as a normal assignment for your magazine."

Nodding her head in acknowledgement, Adebi Adewumi tried to organise her thoughts as if for an ordinary assignment. She caught Paul's attention and discussed the interview schedule with him. Satisfied that this boy was more than capable of posing the challenging questions that he had created, she glanced at her watch and smiled. Joe Bertolli got up, crossed his fingers and made his farewells. "See you back here in about an hour."

Adebi and Paul walked side-by-side across the road and headed towards the barbican of Jericho Castle. They would be just in time for their appointment at Old Heritage Holdings HQ, in the castle keep.

Chapter 17

Ms Perkins Dazzles

Pacing awkwardly in her stiletto heels across the parquet floor of her office, Julia Perkins felt a sense of growing excitement at the imminent arrival of the two interviewers from *History Revealed*. She felt a sense of deep pride that she would appear in this well-regarded magazine. It would be a bonus if she could persuade them that she was really a misunderstood philanthropist who wanted the best for children and young people. She would have to take every opportunity that presented itself to get this message across.

Julia Perkins was dressed in a sober navy blue trouser suit, aiming to create an impression of high-minded seriousness. Her over-laid sheen of pink lipstick and bejewelled earrings were the only clues to the more glamorous and self-absorbed aspects of her character. Glancing at her watch, she flicked her hair as she stole one last look at the body-length mirror attached to her office door. She was ready now and filled with confidence in the knowledge that her one-time buddies were away from headquarters for the day. It'll soon be time to dazzle the two reporters!

By the time she tore herself out of the hypnotic spell induced by admiring herself in the mirror, there was an insistent rap on her door. It was David Roberts, the security guard.

"Ms Adewumi and Master Kanner to see you Ms Perkins. Shall I show them in?"

Julia Perkins nodded her assent and seated herself in her generously padded executive chair. *David Roberts really needs to get that gammy leg of his fixed. His limp is worse than ever! God knows what visitors to the castle think!* With that brief interlude to spare a thought for a fellow-human being, Julia Perkins rose elegantly from her seat to greet her two guests with her most winning smile.

"So lovely to have you visit me here! I so admire your writing for *History Revealed* Adebi...is it alright to call you by your first name?" Not going through the inconvenience of waiting for a reply, Julia Perkins continued unabashed. "As I was saying, it's a wonderful magazine and I'm a big fan. I know it's for kids but I've been reading it for years. Which reminds me, I must get a subscription for my nephew and niece. So, Adebi...and Paul is it? If I understand the purpose of your visit correctly, you'd like to find out all about our wonderful work at Jericho Castle. Let me begin with a little history lesson. You may well know..."

A sense of gloom descended upon Paul Kanner which turned into full-blown vertigo when he felt Julia Perkins's gaze upon him. His eyes rooted to the floor, Paul tried to clear his mind of all the loud sounds and dazzling lights that her voice evoked. Sensing Paul's disquiet, Adebi Adewumi stepped in to rescue the awkward situation created by Ms Perkins's effusive onslaught. "Er...thank you for your kind words...er...Julia... and the historical background. We're delighted to be here and very grateful to you for agreeing to the interview."

The awkward silence that followed was eventually broken by Julia Perkins's show of dazzling teeth, which gave the appearance of something half way between a smile and a grimace. "Good, good. So, shall we proceed? Fire away with your first question!"

Adebi Adewumi put on her most open and friendly face as she began to go through a series of questions that were aimed at relaxing her interviewee and putting her off the scent of anything underhand. Paul's questions would be more probing, but Adebi hoped that coming from a child, they'd be perceived as less threatening. Adebi and Paul had already worked out their strategy: Adebi would ask several general questions about Julia Perkins's career as well as the history of Jericho Castle and these would be interspersed among Paul's "more interesting" questions. Adebi would write brief notes on the answers as Julia Perkins had refused them permission to make an audio recording of the interview.

Ms Perkins dazzled as she answered Adebi's questions at great length. In contrast, she stumbled her way through her answers to Paul's questions:-

"What was your main reason for buying Jericho Castle?"

"What new things do you want to create here to improve kids' learning experience?"

"There are rumours of rare manuscripts hidden in the castle. Do you think these rumours are true?"

"Why have there been so many accidents at the castle?"

Paul's second question was particularly telling as it was met by a blank stare and a mumbled "we're always improving." Clearly, the educational

183

possibilities of Jericho Castle were not at the top of Julia Perkins's agenda. Her answer to Paul's third question was to Adebi's mind aimed at enticing child readers of the magazine. "Well Paul, throughout history, treasure, rare manuscripts and other mysteries have been associated with castles. I wonder what the readers of *History Revealed* think? Come to think of it, there are *so many* rumours of treasure hidden here at Jericho Castle, I am beginning to think they are true...or maybe were true in the past. Maybe your readers can come here and find out for themselves! I myself have spent many hours exploring the chapel...so atmospheric! After our chat, you should go and look around. Mr Roberts the security guard will accompany you."

While Paul struggled somewhat to decode the exact grandstanding intentions of Julia Perkins, he was nonetheless clear in his own mind that she was not being logically consistent. *Her answers seemed to suggest that she cared a lot about history and the*

educational uses of Jericho Castle and yet she had no
ideas or plans worthy of mention. It didn't make any
sense. Did she really care?

Ms Perkins's answer to Paul's final question left
both Paul and Adebi in a state of utter confusion.
"Well now Paul, that *is* a good question. I think you'll
find that many of the kids who come here are of
the...shall we say...adventurous type? So they get
excited in this inspiring environment and try things
out that they shouldn't. Of course, we are improving
things a lot by investing more in structural repairs
and so on. I think you'll find that the rate of accidents
is going down all the time and before long we'll have
very few accidents." This answer was delivered with
a self-satisfied smile and in the face of an incredulous
pair of interviewers. *The number of accidents has not*
decreased was Paul Kanner's last thought before the
interview was brought to an abrupt end.

"Alas, our fifty minutes is up! Thank you Adebi
and Paul for a most enjoyable interview. I look

forward to reading it in the magazine. Ah, here's Mr Roberts!"

Walking back towards the barbican in the shadow of a very attentive David Roberts, Adebi looked straight ahead while Paul bent down momentarily to tie an errant shoe-lace. The one-hundred metre walk to the portcullis, the gateway to the world beyond this oppressive place, seemed to take an age. Adebi and Paul could not wait to shake off Mr Roberts and the dust of Jericho Castle.

Joe Bertolli hovered anxiously outside by the entrance of the café. He waved at Paul and Adebi as soon as they appeared through the open portcullis.

"Let's get you two a drink first and then you can tell me all about what you've discovered from Ms Perkins."

While Adebi provided a brief summary of Ms Perkins's answers, Paul fiddled with a piece of paper distractedly.

"It sounds as though she didn't buy into Jericho

Castle in order to enhance kids' lives or out of concern for maintaining the cultural heritage. So why did she do it?" Joe Bertolli looked for some seconds in Paul's direction. Realising that Paul had not picked up on his cue, he smiled and coughed pointedly. "Hey Paul! You seem a little distracted. I was just asking why Ms Perkins invested money in Jericho Castle."

"Er...she said it seemed like a good idea at the time and her two friends encouraged her. Because she's keen on history as well it seemed it was 'fated to be'. I...er...didn't really understand her reasons." Paul hung his head and looked at his shoes, his face reddening in the process."

"Well you know what Paul, she didn't make sense to me either! I didn't understand half her answers. I think she was using the interview as a vehicle for her own ends." Adebi then turned her attention to Joe.

"Joe, I don't know what you were expecting to

gain from the interview but I can tell you that she was the most elusive person I've ever interviewed. She obviously relishes the idea of her account appearing in my magazine...a bit of free self-promotion."

Joe Bertolli smiled wryly. "Thanks to you and Paul, the interview tells me everything that I need to know. The dazzling Ms Perkins is hiding something. I now know we're on the right track."

Sheepishly, Paul looked up. "Erm...I found this."

Chapter 18

Dropping a Clanger

Joe Bertolli and Adebi Adewumi stared at the small object nestled in Paul Kanner's hand. Joe wondered whether Paul had filched an incriminating object from Julia Perkins's office. He gazed at an unflinching Paul for some seconds before slowly reaching out to grasp the object.

"A cufflink...with...the de Courcy coat of arms! Where did you find this Paul?"

"I found it on the path just outside Ms Perkins's office door. I noticed something bright on the ground and decided to pick it up. I hadn't seen it before on our way in. The man...the security guard, Mr Roberts, kept looking at me so I decided to re-tie my shoelace so that I wouldn't get into trouble."

"That's a great find Paul! Maybe this cufflink belonged to the missing historian Marcus Beard. Maybe they've held him as a prisoner at the castle...he must know something that they want kept under wraps. We know that Dr Beard is a member of the de Courcy family and we know that he seemed to have more than a passing interest in Jericho Castle. It all makes sense!"

Adebi's puzzled expression froze Joe's self-satisfied grin. "Sorry Joe, I don't understand what you're saying! Do you mean that the three people behind Old Heritage Holdings have abducted and imprisoned a historian for several years because he knew too much?"

A note of uncertainty crept into Joe Bertolli's voice as the starkness of Adebi's question jolted something in his brain. "Er...yes! I think something like this has taken place. Maybe not all three owners knew or were involved...maybe just Julia Perkins...or maybe just the other two, Patrick Leyton and Victoria Singh. I'm also deeply suspicious of that security guard...he is probably the general dogsbody of whoever is the brains behind all this. We need more evidence, but I think we're on the right track." Joe's voice trailed off to a low pleading whine by the time he had uttered the last few words. Already, his mind was beginning to fill with nagging doubts, though he didn't know why."

While Adebi continued to stare at Joe with a face filled with incredulity, Paul Kanner began distractedly to twirl his hair in a very animated way while staring at the cuff-link on the table.

"Erm...I...er...think something else is happening. Er...when we went to see Ms Perkins, there was no cuff-link on the ground. Fifty-two minutes later, when we came out, it was

191

there...er...on the path. Someone was wearing it and they dropped it while we were...er...interviewing Ms Perkins. We need to look for someone in the castle who wears one of those tailored shirts."

Adebi felt that Paul's suggestion was the more practical one. "Right Paul! Julia Perkins said we could have a tour of the castle. Let's go and find Mr David Roberts to escort us around the place. You can keep your eyes peeled for anyone wearing an appropriate shirt while I distract Mr Roberts with chatter. You never know, we might even see someone with a missing cuff-link!"

A peevish Joe Bertolli set his jaw and began to complain that there was only so much coffee a man could drink whilst waiting for amateur sleuths to do a proper detective's job. By the time Joe had finished complaining, Paul and Adebi were out of earshot and within touching distance of the castle's portcullis. It dawned on Joe very suddenly that his only audience were the bemused and staring faces of the café's customers.

As soon as Paul and Adebi entered the barbican through the portcullis they saw the retreating figure of David Roberts. Adebi called after him and quickened her pace to catch up with him. While Paul hung back at the inner end of the barbican, Adebi negotiated a tour with David Roberts.

"...and here we have the chapel. I don't know how much medieval history they teach you in your school...er...Mr Kanner, but castle chapels have a very significant place in history and legend."

Adebi became increasingly concerned that David Roberts was drawing in both Paul and herself, so that neither of them could keep a look-out for people with a tailored shirt with a missing cuff-link. Roberts seemed particularly skilled at capturing their attention whenever they began to focus on a passerby. *Maybe it had something to do with his training as a security guard. Maybe he was suspicious of them. I need to control HIS attention to give Paul a chance of spotting our quarry.*

"This place is so fascinating Mr Roberts! You must get a lot of satisfaction from working here. Tell me, do you have a particular passion for history?"

David Roberts stared with narrowed eyes at Adebi, then turned his attention to Paul before answering Adebi's question. "Well, isn't everyone interested in history? Since I started working here I've watched the odd documentary on castles and medieval history and maybe read a book or two...but I wouldn't say I was passionate." Again, David Roberts's gaze gave an appraising look to both guests before leading them back to the barbican.

"Thank you for such an interesting and informative tour Mr Roberts. I will write to Ms Perkins to say what a wonderful guide you've been." Adebi smiled at the security-guard-cum-tour-guide all the while looking for clues as to what he was thinking or feeling. The man gave nothing away, but

Adebi felt instinctively that he was hiding something. Paul also said his "thank yous" just as David Roberts turned away and skulked back to his domain.

Disheartened by the lack of any obvious progress, Adebi turned her attention to Paul. "Did you see anyone who might fit the bill?" Paul narrowed his eyes and was lost in his own thought processes for some seconds before he slowly shook his head.

An agitated Joe Bertolli eagerly awaited them again in the café doorway. His expectant look soon turned to one of disappointment as he read the faces of his two accomplices.

Chapter 19

Solitary Snooping

Crouching outside in the shadow of the castle wall, Joe Bertolli waited for his main chance to enter the barbican. Last time he was here, he had come as a paying customer and had suffered the consequences of being discovered prowling. He didn't want to take risks on this occasion; he wanted the luxury of spending most of the night in the castle grounds and watching for misdeeds. *Maybe see some clues about the whereabouts of a missing historian!* He was convinced that the security guard, David Roberts, had something to do with the abduction of Dr Marcus Beard as well as a number of other misadventures that had befallen other victims. *I need to get in there and catch him doing something nefarious!*

It was now 18.13 and he was hoping that a

member of staff would open the portcullis to exit the castle and head homeward. If Joe was really clever, he might manage to sneak in unobserved at the same time. Fortunately, Adebi Adewumi, the reporter for *History Revealed*, had agreed to give Paul a lift to his home in Greenwich. Joe could now concentrate unhindered in his quest.

As the minutes ticked away, Joe was beginning to entertain serious doubts about the wisdom of his strategy. *Maybe the staff live on the premises! Maybe all those who go home after a day's work here have already left.* Negative thoughts coalesced with the gloom of darkness to form a puddle of despondency in Joe's brain. *Maybe it's time to call it quits. Get home to a nice cool beer.* Just as the prospect of home comforts and a cold beer began to improve his mood, the sound of rattles and creaks made his senses snap to attention. *This is it!*

Joe drew himself level with the nearside of the portcullis and knelt in the dark. As soon as the

197

portcullis had cleared two feet off the ground, he wriggled through the entrance on his stomach, hoping that he wouldn't collide with whoever was leaving the castle. He heard a female's voice and male laughter coming from the approaching silhouettes. The light was almost non-existent in the barbican but he could make out three figures approaching in his direction. Luckily, they were all walking along the opposite side of the barbican and within a few seconds, were through the portcullis without a backward glance in his direction. *Phew!*

Seconds after gingerly entering the castle bailey, Joe heard the same rattling and creaking sound as before as the portcullis descended shut. It was much darker in the open expanse of the bailey than he'd anticipated. He slowly allowed his vision to adapt to the darkness before raising himself into an upright position. After another couple of minutes spent scanning the various buildings, Joe decided to head for the watchtower at the eastern end of the northern rampart. This was the building that he and Maxine Carter had attempted to investigate last time he was here. The building's position and stature made it the perfect observation post for his snooping.

Continually scanning the dark expanse of the castle grounds, Joe shuffled his way to the watchtower. With his back to the wall, he let out a sigh of relief that he'd made it unnoticed. He now turned his attention to the window through which he'd helped Maxine Carter in their previous sortie. *Damn it!* Joe gazed at the now-sealed window and experienced the odd sensation of mental and physical deflation. The window was encased in an impenetrable steel plate. He now felt like a popped balloon. Minutes earlier, he'd had it all mapped out: *the security guard was in cahoots with at least one of the owners of Old Heritage Holdings and was keeping the historian Marcus Beard somewhere in the castle. The watchtower would be the ideal place as it is*

secure and the top floor is out of bounds to visitors.
*Marcus Beard must know something...*His thoughts
were interrupted by the violent rattling and creaking
of the portcullis. Someone was coming into the
castle grounds.

Joe got down on his haunches and then crept
on hands and knees towards the chapel. Keeping
low, he reached a corner of the chapel. A torchlight
was bobbing up and down and seemed to be on
course for the watchtower. Feeling as though his
racing heart-rate would soon reach its limit, Joe
forced himself to focus on the ghostly outlines of the
torch-bearer. He couldn't make anything out; just a
smudge of black that was now unlocking the door to
the watchtower with heavy clanking sounds.

The door was still ajar as the faint beam of light
retreated into the interior of the building. Joe
stealthily crept towards the entrance, but as he
reached for the door, he heard a cough at close
quarters followed by a sigh of exasperation and a

challenging voice..."Hello! Anyone there? Is it you Helen, playing silly buggers again?" Retreating from the doorway as quietly as he could, Joe recognised the voice as that of the security guard, David Roberts. When he'd previously heard the security guard speak, Joe had a faint suspicion that the man was putting on the exaggerated London accent, a little like an American actor trying to sound Cockney. Before Joe could conclude his ruminations on the security guard, he was distracted by another bobbing beam of light coming from the other side of the keep.

"Hi Dave! Got you the sarnies and coffee...come and get 'em!"

David Roberts grabbed what Joe assumed were sandwiches and a flask of coffee from the young woman. "Thanks Helen, you're a star. Go home if you like... won't be here much longer. Little job I gotta do then off home. By the way, don't bother trying to pull another prank like you did on Monday...I'm busy and want to get home."

As Helen retreated, the door to the watchtower slammed shut and Joe heard David Roberts clambering up the stairs, whistling the tune of *Rule Britannia* as he went.

Retreating to the shadows, Joe kept his eyes and ears focused on what was going on within the walls of the watchtower. Joe realised that the impenetrable walls would reveal very few signs of what was going on inside. *It's going to be a long night!*

Joe decided to use this hiatus as an opportunity to snoop around the place. He climbed up the ramparts to the place where Paul Kanner's classmate Lisa Khan had fallen...which of course was also the place where Benjamin Zeigarnik had been coshed. He tiptoed toward the dark mass that was the watchtower at the end of the rampart and turned on his 'phone's flashlight. Maybe he could find a way into the building from up here. In front of him was an arched wooden door approximately four feet in height. Joe got up close to the door to inspect for any gaps between the jamb and the door. He noted instead the two large metal brackets with padlocks at the top and bottom of the door. *Very suspicious...and very promising! Something valuable must be stored in here!* In his youth, he'd often played at lock-picking with his mates, but was never any good at it. In fact, neither were his mates! *The only way in is to remove the padlocks. If only I had some tools!*

Scratching his head furiously in the hope of dredging up a solution, Joe decided to go down to the bailey and look for some loose bricks or stones that he could use to lever the brackets off the door. Just as he reached the bottom of the stairs, a resounding slam came from the direction of the ground-floor door. Evidently, David Roberts had finished his "little job"...*probably feeding the imprisoned Marcus Beard and giving him a little pep-*

talk!

As the security guard's footsteps receded, Joe felt compelled to visit the watchtower entrance one last time. Taking out his 'phone flashlight again, he sought for weak-points in the door and locks. Giving up and about to turn off the 'phone, Joe spotted a small edge of heightened reflectivity at the bottom of the door; something that looked white. Leaning down, he managed to make contact using the tip of his little-finger. Very slowly, he clawed with a finger-nail as millimetre by millimetre the white edge revealed itself to be a piece of paper.

Cupping his hand round the 'phone, Joe gazed at the paper with eyes wide with amazement. It was a letter...and handwritten on very fancy paper! He couldn't believe his luck. *That idiot David Roberts must have dropped this...proof that Marcus Beard has been held captive! Something to entice Hertfordshire Police Force!*

Gray's Inn
Gray's Inn Square
London WC1R 5JA

January 19th 2015

Dr Marcus Beard
School of History
University of Kent
Canterbury CT2 7NZ

Dear Dr Beard,

Thank you for your letter of December 23rd, 2014. Excuse my tardy reply but the festive season has left me the worse for wear and consequently playing catch-up with legal affairs and correspondence.

While I sympathise with your plight, I cannot in all conscience offer you much hope in pursuance of what you consider to be your rightful inheritance. As explained in previous correspondence, your great-great-grandfather, Guy de Courcy was very particular and explicit in the terms of his will concerning the fate of Jericho Castle. I emphasise once again that Old Heritage Holdings are the legal and rightful owners of Jericho Castle.

You mention that you are privy to certain delicate details concerning the contents of the castle which might present a new legal challenge to the terms of ownership by Old Heritage Holdings. I must say I cannot envision any circumstances that would present a serious legal challenge to the ownership of the castle by Old Heritage Holding. Having said that, if you were more forthcoming about the alleged contents of the castle I may be able to take a different perspective on this matter.

I am very sorry to hear that you have been terminated by the university. These are difficult times indeed. I wish you every success in the future and hope you find your pot of gold at the end of the rainbow. Best wishes for the new year.

Yours sincerely,

JUqhrt

James Urquhart QC

Chapter 20

Storming the Ramparts

Detective Chief Inspector Maria Kelly followed on Joe Bertolli's heels as he approached the portcullis of Jericho Castle. DCI Kelly was really excited to have been the recipient of Sgt Bertolli's tip-off about the suspect David Roberts, but was also very embarrassed. The Metropolitan Police sergeant had tried to alert her team at Hertfordshire Police some time ago, but was repeatedly rebuffed. *If only they'd taken his concerns more seriously...but then again, it was down to his boss. DCI Sara Gravesham informed her that Bertolli was quirky and not a team player, but then only most recently admitted that he had an excellent track record in solving serious crimes.*

Looking up in the direction of the chinking sound of grappling hooks as they made contact with the battlements, Maria Kelly felt a visceral thrill. The night sky was moonless which added to her feeling that something mischievous could pop out of the air. She had always loved mysteries and adventures, from her early days of reading *The Famous Five* stories under the bedcovers, to her student and police cadet days when she would spend weekends exploring caves, rock- climbing and wandering through old ruins. Aged 47, and more-or-less desk-bound, she was no longer the fit and lithe figure of her youth. When she sat at her desk to plan this raid on the castle, she knew that she would have to be a part of it.

After three uniformed police officers had managed to scramble over the battlements and onto the rampart, DCI Maria Kelly raised her foot on the first wrung of the rope-ladder. As she pulled her weight off the ground, the ladder, with her foot still on it, began to rotate perilously. DCI Kelly came to earth with a crash as Joe Bertolli wondered how this senior officer had acquired the nickname of "Keep-Fit-Kelly". As Joe bent down to help, Maria Kelly flung her arm backwards, felling him in the process. Seconds later, Joe Bertolli and Maria Kelly were rolling with laughter at the absurdity of the situation: England's finest crime-fighters couldn't even manage to stand up straight!

An urgent screech brought both police officers back to their senses. It sounded like a shriek of terror...only more shrill. Bertolli and Kelly looked at one another just in time for the sound to be repeated. "We'd better get in there Sergeant!" Dusting themselves off, the two police officers ambled to the portcullis, and looked through the barbican for signs of activity within the castle grounds. It was pitch-black and deathly quiet. DCI Maria Kelly was really beginning to enjoy a rush of adrenaline; Sgt Joe Bertolli was not.

The silence was suddenly broken by a louder screech that was heading towards them. A second later, they could just about make out the form of a white bird gliding over the castle wall and heading towards the woodland behind them. A relieved Joe Bertolli decided that it was probably a barn owl. Before Joe could say anything, Maria Kelly ordered Joe Bertolli to climb up the castle wall and report back to her on what was going on.

Joe reluctantly followed his orders, taking three times as long as the uniformed police to reach the battlements above. From the vantage point of the rampart, Joe narrowed his eyes and scanned the bailey for signs of movement...nothing! The castle was shrouded in silence.

Inching his way down the stairs, Joe stopped periodically to listen for sounds. Reaching the bailey, he cast around for signs of the three uniformed policemen who had preceded him into the grounds. He saw a faint glow of light behind the silhouetted door of the castle keep in the centre of the castle grounds and decided to make his way there. In previous visits, he'd made a mental note to explore the keep, but never got round to it. After all, the security guard David Roberts seemed always to be scurrying around the watchtower at the end of the northern rampart. *Roberts must have more than one secret location.* Scanning the majestic height of the keep walls he spotted an even fainter light in a narrow window near the top. *Aha!*

Ambling towards the keep in a crouched position, Joe tried to suppress his growing anxieties about what he might encounter in the there. Focusing hard on the doorway ahead, he suddenly found himself sprawled on the floor, having tripped over what felt like a sandbag. His whispered curses gave way to curiosity about the offending object. Groping the object gingerly, he came to the realisation that it was a body! As he explored the prone figure with the palms of his hands he came into contact with what was obviously a set of handcuffs. *This must be one of the uniforms that came in earlier!* It took some seconds for Joe to locate the victim's wrist and feel for a pulse. He could just make out a pulse, though he had to check this several times in case he had imagined it. *He's definitely alive but his pulse is week.* Joe was in a quandary: *should he go back and inform DCI Kelly so that the policeman could receive medical attention? But then, the other two policemen might be in danger in the castle keep!*

While his inner conflict raged on, Joe's legs were less ambivalent and took him steadily and directly to the door of the keep. He nervously crept up the steps to the first landing, then peered into the gloom of the ascending stairway. The darkness was complete by the time he had reached the second landing. Getting low on his hands and knees, he groped his way up the stairs, feeling the rounded edge of each cold stone step as he went. When he reached midway between the third and fourth landings he heard a slamming sound from above followed immediately by the dancing appearance of nearby torchlight. Bracing himself, Joe tried to retrace his steps backward, anxious not to make a sound. Before he managed three retreating steps, he found himself in the full beam of an anonymous torchlight.

At last Sarge! What kept you?" The uniformed policeman motioned with his torch as Joe followed him to the fourth landing. Once he'd reached the landing, Joe made out a dimly lit recess to the right and followed his colleague there. He could now make out more of the detail as his vision adapted to the gloomy conditions: an open security gate behind which stood a door, slightly ajar, with the words **Armoury and Storeroom** emblazoned on the top. As they entered the room, lit up by an overhead lamp, Joe could see the prone figure of David Roberts, handcuffed arms behind his back and a scowling expression on his face.

~~~~~~~~~~

On this cold Saturday afternoon they were all
rubbing their hands in front of the open hearth at
The Chandos pub in the heart of London's West End
near Trafalgar Square. Joe Bertolli was determined to
celebrate solving the Jericho Castle case and to this
end, had arranged for cabs to pick up each of his
friends from their home and bring them directly to
the pub. Though he would not admit it to anyone, he
was particularly pleased by his boss DCI Sara
Gravesham's plaudits. DCI Maria Kelly of the
Hertfordshire Police Force was effusive in her praise
of Joe's breakthrough and had called DCI Gravesham
to thank her profusely for lending her this
outstanding detective.

Silently looking at his friends, Joe reflected on
the part they each played in solving this tortuous
case. Paul Kanner briefly met his gaze and smiled for
an instant before returning his brooding attention to

the warming flames of the fire.

"I just want to say 'thank you' to each and every one of you for helping to solve this case. Without you, God alone knows how many more injuries and deaths would Jericho Castle witness before it was finally shut down. Cheers!"

Benjamin Zeigarnik, Maxine Carter and Luigi Pecorino returned Joe's salutation and were warming to the celebratory atmosphere that Joe had created so close to Christmas. Paul Kanner stood out from the group: nursing a Coke in one hand and a burger in the other, he continued to gaze into the dancing flames. He turned once again to look at Joe and was about to speak when a sudden draft of cold air disturbed the cosy atmosphere around the hearth.

"Hi Joe, hi Paul. Sorry I'm late!" Adebi Adewumi flounced to the table and sat next to her old university mentor, Luigi Pecorino, with whom she immediately began to reminisce happily about the old days.

"Now that we're all here, I'd like to fill you in on what we know about the security guard, David Roberts." Joe held their gaze as he went on to recount the key details. David Roberts was pursued to the castle keep after he'd bludgeoned unconscious a pursuing policeman. He was eventually found hiding in the armoury and storeroom off the fourth landing of the castle keep. The room contained a number of items appearing to belong to Marcus Beard, the missing historian, including letters from friends, colleagues and legal advisers. The Hertfordshire police also impounded a laptop that appeared to belong to Marcus Beard, as the cover was adorned with two stickers bearing the de Courcy coat of arms. The police have so far failed to crack the laptop's password.

Another disturbing discovery is that "David Roberts" is an assumed name. Hertfordshire Police found hundreds of official records of people named

'David Roberts', but none had any other details that matched with those of the security guard. Further investigations revealed that his employment as a security guard by Old Heritage Holdings was in breach of employment legislation and his pay had not been declared for tax purposes. One of the owners of Jericho Castle, Julia Perkins, who was recently interviewed by Paul and Adebi for *History Revealed*, claimed to the police that David Roberts was hired through a recruitment agency called "Safety Shield" who handled his contract and pay. The police could find no trace of this agency.

"So Joe, this dodgy man is doing dodgy work for a dodgy organisation. What do you think they're up to?" Benjamin Zeigarnik wore a smirk of satisfaction as he enjoyed throwing this challenging question in the direction of the previously smug Joe Bertolli.

"Well, it's clear that 'David Roberts' is behind a lot of the incidents at the castle and was certainly behind the disappearance of Marcus Beard. Large bottles of sulphuric acid were found in a locked cupboard in the storeroom and there is forensic evidence that some of the stone steps and metal security railings around the castle had been corroded by acid. He obviously wanted to scare off inquisitive minds. My guess is that Beard was kept in the armoury and storeroom for some time. We found a cot-bed there as well as stores of food and drink. 'Roberts' must have recently moved him elsewhere, probably in response to our recent sorties. I would also guess that Julia Perkins is the mastermind behind all this. She must be worried that Marcus Beard has a claim on the castle or knows something that would incriminate her. She probably hired 'Roberts' to do her dirty work for her. The thing is, he won't say a word and just stares into space every time he's questioned."

While Benjamin was not fully satisfied with Joe's answer, he decided to allow others to join the discussion. He cast a glance at the particularly distracted and quiet Paul Kanner. "Hey Paul my friend. Would you like to say something to Joe? You've met this 'David Roberts' and Julia Perkins at close quarters. Do you think they're hiding something?"

"Erm...I don't know. Mr Roberts is very unfriendly and was in a hurry when he showed us round the castle...er...a bit scary. Miss Perkins confused me. She wanted to be in Adebi's magazine. She said things that didn't...make sense."

As Benjamin nodded his head in support, the other members of the group began to chatter in the hope of regaining the earlier festive mood. After all, Sgt Joe Bertolli's assessment was probably correct. Even though more evidence was needed, it would surely be just a matter of time before the man who called himself 'David Roberts' was brought to book...and maybe even the elusive Miss Perkins.

Amid all the merriment, Paul Kanner continued

to feel agitated and unsettled. He repeatedly flipped between two images on his smart-phone. Something in these two images had been bothering him on and off for some days. As he twirled his hair, he began to sigh in frustration. Benjamin Zeigarnik continued to register concern on his face as he watched Paul go through an agonised search for a resolution. Suddenly, Paul's eyes widened and he looked pointedly in Joe Bertolli's direction, mouth agape.

"Look! I think I've found something!"

The assembled friends all turned towards Paul as he raised his mobile 'phone and turned the screen toward them. Joe Bertolli got up from his seat to get a closer look.

"What is it Paul?" Paul showed Joe a photo of the security guard, David Roberts, followed by the old photo of the historian Marcus Beard. "What are you trying to tell me Paul? I know who they are."

"No...look...the nose!"

Joe Bertolli forced himself to examine the nose

of each of the two men. After some seconds, Joe lifted his head, a bewildered look splayed across his face. "Erm...everyone take a look...I think I er...got it wrong."

As each of them took a turn to examine the photos on Paul's 'phone, Joe continued to scratch his head in disbelief and embarrassment. The collective silence from the others shattered the earlier celebratory mood once and for all.

It was now time to face new facts. "Well done Paul. You made the discovery, so you can explain it to everyone."

Paul Kanner was unused to commanding the attention of any group of people, much less one of such accomplished adults. He gazed at the table to avoid being distracted and took some seconds to marshal his thoughts.

"It began three days ago during my school lunch-break. I was thinking that Mr Roberts the security guard at Jericho Castle reminded me of someone else. So...er...I took out my 'phone to look at the picture of him I took on my second visit to the castle. I couldn't think who he reminded me of even when I looked for a long time at his picture. When I got home after school...er...I...had a bad thought about the missing historian, Dr Beard. I...er...had this thought telling me he is dead. It was scary. I looked at the old photo of him in his office that I found online nine weeks ago and...*he* reminded me of someone too!

I've been looking at the two photos at least eight times every day since and...er...it was just now that I noticed that they both had the...er...same nose! Near the right nostril they both have a small crescent-shaped scar...and er...on the bridge of the nose, they both have a little black mole. I thought it was some kind of printing flaw at first, but then when I saw they were both exactly the same...I...er realised. Mr Roberts is Dr Marcus!"

Joe Bertolli broke the stunned silence that

ensued. "The two faces differ quite a bit at first glance, but then they were taken a number of years apart and maybe 'David Roberts' has taken pains to disguise some of his original features." Joe turned his gaze to Maxine Carter, who nodded in anticipation of his request.

"I'm on it Joe. I'll feed the photos into the face-matching software back at the station."

Chapter 21

Case Solved?

A woman dressed in a woolly bob-hat and trench-coat stood in the shadows opposite *Café Roma* in Bloomsbury in the centre of London. The dark December night concealed everything about her intentions, except perhaps the object of her gaze, which was a scruffy looking car in an adjacent alleyway. Unbeknown to the occupants, they were the special object of interest to this shadowy figure.

Joe Bertolli was the last person to emerge from the car, having been left behind by his three passengers who were already across the street and at the threshold of Luigi Pecorino's restaurant. Joe had given a lift to Paul Kanner, Maxine Carter and Benjamin Zeigarnik and they were running fifteen minutes late for their dinner appointment with Luigi and Adebi. Joe was completely unaware of the statuesque woman in the nearby shadows.

The restaurant exuded warmth, comfort and cheer and Joe was happy to join his friends at a large round table that had been reserved for them by Luigi. He couldn't wait to tell everyone about what had developed since they last met as a group.

"I know we're running late and you must all be starving, but I'd like to give you a quick update on the Jericho Castle case before we eat. Unsurprisingly, Maxine's computer-analysis of the two photographs suggested that David Roberts and Marcus Beard are probably one and the same person. I informed DCI Kelly of the Hertfordshire Police and she obtained permission for me to be involved in re-interviewing David Roberts. When he was confronted with the revelation that we knew that he was really Marcus Beard, he went into a rant about how his heritage had been stolen and how he should be the rightful owner of Jericho Castle. I should point out that at this point his accent changed: less 'Cockney' and more 'refined'.

Marcus Beard's self-righteous indignation continued unabated, until I reminded him of the fatality and the injuries that he had caused. Surprisingly, he stopped protesting and looked guilty and crestfallen. He merely said that he hadn't meant for things to have gone so far. When I brought up the tragedy of Paul's classmate Lisa Khan, he looked quite distraught and even shed a tear. To his credit, he hung his head in shame. But the poor girl will need more than Beard's guilt to get her life back on track.

There's a lot that we still don't know about Marcus Beard's activities and the extent to which he had been aided or goaded by others. What he volunteered was that from early childhood, his mother had told him that one day he would become the owner of Jericho Castle. His lifelong interest in history began early and culminated in his pursuing an academic career as a historian.

From the age of 16 he became particularly engrossed in his forebears' legacy and spent considerable time visiting and researching castles in general and Jericho Castle in particular. Whilst a history student at university, he had created a grand plan of how Jericho Castle could be used as a centre for history education, using hands-on and virtual reality displays to bring history alive for kids.

By the time he was 22 years of age, he realised that all his dreams would never materialise. It was at this point in his life that he understood that he would not be able to inherit the castle without considerable financial backing. His academic career was slowly progressing, but by the time he was in his late-twenties, his life began to unravel. His friends began to distance themselves from him as they found him to be too obsessive. His girlfriend left him for the same reason. His university sacked him after two written warnings for failing to carry out his teaching duties adequately.

With little left to lose, he got himself a new identity as "David Roberts" and got himself a job as a security guard at the castle. At least that way he could keep an eye on the place and make sure the new owners, Old Heritage Holdings, did not turn the place into some awful theme park. He also admitted that he made up his own 'recruitment agency' so that he could apply for the job and receive payment without having to show proof of his identity. That's about all we know about him. He even refused to explain why he had some personal effects stored in the castle and why he slept there...though it's easy to guess why."

In the silence that followed, everyone forgot their hunger as each person tried in their own unique way to make sense of what they had just heard. Luigi Pecorino hesitantly broke the silence.

"Tell me Joe. Does this Marcus Beard claim that he sabotaged parts of the castle to stop the owners from getting on with planned changes?"

"No Luigi. He's refusing to answer any questions on his activities in the castle."

Benjamin Zeigarnik began to drum his fingers in agitation on the table. "Joe, I wish you got me involved in the interview process. I keep telling you that empathy is the key. Show that you can understand someone and they will open up to you! I guess you forgot all my advice from previous cases!"

"Benjamin, Benjamin, Benjamin...you love to make me appear like some kind of inept Neanderthal! We got as far as we did in the interview precisely because I followed your advice. I even told him that I was sure he didn't intend for anyone to get hurt, much less lose their lives. I told him I could relate to his feelings of being dispossessed and let down by friends. I think I developed a good rapport with him."

Adebi looked at the puzzled faces around the table and decided to throw in one of her own speculations. "If Marcus Beard did not challenge the accusation that he caused injury and death, then he might be guarding a secret of even greater importance to him. Maybe he does know about valuable items secretly stored within the castle."

"Or maybe he's covering up for someone!" replied Maxine Carter, who agreed with Joe's initial assessment that someone at Old Heritage Holdings was in on this.

The incomplete and unsatisfying conclusion to the case cast a gloom around the table that began to rival the darkness outside.

"Time to get some food and drink my friends." Luigi forced a smile as he proffered menus to his guests. "It is an indisputable fact that it is impossible to think clearly on an empty stomach! Anyway, we need to cheer up and enjoy the successes we've had. We now have our man and the misadventures at Jericho Castle have surely come to an end."

The mood lightened immediately as the meals were delivered to the table. Smiles appeared as the aroma of linguine vongole competed with those of breaded veal and pizza. As the wine flowed conversations about Christmas began to predominate over their earlier concerns about crime-solving. Before long, the gloom of the earlier part of the evening was left far behind.

Joe looked at his friends and raised his wine glass. "I propose a toast. To Luigi and his marvellous restaurant! May they both live long and prosper... and of course, to the one and only Paul! Without you, we wouldn't be here!"

The resounding cheers galvanised Adebi, who began to regale her new friends with funny stories of Luigi's exploits when he was a younger man, teaching history at the university. She reminded Luigi of the time he raced into the lecture theatre wearing his chef's checkered trousers and a smouldering tie. While Luigi smiled in embarrassment, Paul Kanner peered through the window at the silhouette of a stranger across the street.

Afterword

Paul Kanner's name was derived from Dr Leo Kanner, the Austrian-American child psychiatrist who first identified child autism in 1943. A clear account of the man and his work is available in this article:

Cohmer, S. (2014). Autistic disturbances of affective contact (1943), by Leo Kanner. http://embryo.asu.edu/handle/10776/7895

Paul has Asperger's Syndrome, which shares some features with autism. This is named after Hans Asperger, an Austrian Paediatrician who identified the syndrome in 1944. His life has been surrounded by controversy, with some accounts lauding him as a saviour of children during the Nazi atrocities while others have implicated him as a Nazi collaborator. Indeed, some authors argue that using the term "Asperger's Syndrome" pays undue homage to the man:

Czech, H. (2018), Hans Asperger, national socialism, and 'race hygiene' in Nazi-era Vienna. *Molecular Autism, 9:29.*

https://molecularautism.biomedcentral.com/articles/10.1186/s13229-018-0208-6

Sher, D.A. (2020). The aftermath of the Hans Asperger exposé. *The Psychologist*, September issue, pp 76-79. https://thepsychologist.bps.org.uk/volume-33/september-2020/aftermath-hans-asperger-expose

It is noteworthy that the term "Asperger's Syndrome" was discontinued as a diagnostic label by the American Psychiatric Association in 2013 and was subsumed under the more generic term "Autism Spectrum Disorder". However, the original term is still in general currency.

For accounts of psychological characteristics of people with Asperger's Syndrome:

Robison, J.E. (2007). *Look Me in the Eye*. NY: Crown Books.

Silberman, S. (2015). *Neurotribes*. London: Allen & Unwin.

For children: Jennifer Cook O'Toole's *The Asperkid's (Secret) Book of Social Rules*, published by Jessica Kingsley Publishers.

Dr Benjamin Zeigarnik was named after Dr Bluma Zeigarnik, a psychologist who had studied and qualified in Berlin before returning to her homeland in the Soviet Union, where she worked in various university departments, clinics and research institutes. She was affiliated with Moscow State University until 1988, the year of her death, aged 81! She was a pioneer in the fields of memory research and clinical psychology in the 1920s and 1930s and has a very memorable Russian-sounding name! I see Benjamin as a fictional grandson of Bluma. An account of her life and work can be found in:

Zeigarnik, A.V. (2007). Bluma Zeigarnik: A memoir. *Gestalt Theory, 29(3)*, 256-268. http://www.gestalttheory.net/cms/uploads/pdf/GTH -Archive/2007Zeigarnik_Memoir.pdf

Jericho Castle is a fiction, but **Arundel Castle**, on which it is modelled has existed for over 900 years. A Norman castle at the edge of the town of Arundel in Sussex, it was established on Christmas Day 1067 by Roger de Montgomery, through the graces of William the Conqueror. Its current owner is the Duke of Norfolk.

Guy de Courcy is also fictional. I chose what at the time appeared to be a random process a name that seemed typically Norman. As luck would have it, several Guy de Courcys existed in the past and continue to exist to this day. The de Courcy heraldry depicted in this book is authentic and goes back to the 12th century.

The Ames Distorted Room along with other visual illusions is described and explained in various websites, where you can even access instructions for building your own small-scale Distorted Room! https://www.pinterest.co.uk/pin/457537643365524971/?nic_v2=1axoDpXuS Richard Gregory's book *Eye and Brain*, originally published in 1966 by World University Press, is a psychology classic and continues to be a useful primer on visual illusions. It is available in several newer editions.

Bullies and Humour: Dr Benjamin Zeigarnik periodically provides informal and discreet advice to Paul Kanner on how to cope with being bullied and devalued. In this book, Paul implements Benjamin's suggestion to confound his enemies with humour and the unexpected.

Evidence indicates that children and adolescents with Autism Spectrum Disorders (ASD) are more likely to be the victims of both verbal and physical bullying than their peers. Research and common experience suggest that bullies are often motivated by the desire to dominate and humiliate others in order to be popular among an "in-crowd". Bullies frequently target peers who are "different" or show signs of being vulnerable, and it is therefore both unfortunate and unsurprising that people with ASD are targeted by bullies. Recent evidence suggests that the degree of bullying experienced by ASD adolescents is correlated with the extent to which they show signs of emotional vulnerability, such as anxiety:

Tipton-Fisler, L.A. et al. (2018). Stability of bullying and internalising problems among adolescents with ASD, ID, or typical development. *Research in Developmental Disabilities, 80,* 131-141. https://www.researchgate.net/publication/3264649 43_Stability_of_bullying_and_internalizing_problems _among_adolescents_with_ASD_ID_or_typical_devel opment

Benjamin as a psychologist is very aware of this issue and his advice is underpinned by four reasons:

1. Making jokes can reduce signs of anxiety that an individual might display, thereby making the individual appear less vulnerable and hence less likely to be targeted.

2. Making jokes can frustrate the bully's expected "pay-off" of cowering a victim and so bullying the victim becomes less rewarding.

3. Laughter and anger or aggression are often (but not always!) incompatible

emotional states. Humour may change the bully's mind-set at a crucial moment and make it less likely that s/he will escalate hostilities.

4. Being humorous gains the individual greater acceptance among peers in general, who become potential allies against the bully.

While there is little scientific evidence that Benjamin's prescription is useful, several authors have included humour in their advice to victims of bullying:

Marano, H.E. (2010). Top strategies for handling a bully. *Psychology Today* (online). https://www.psychologytoday.com/gb/blog/brainstorm/201003/top-strategies-handling-bully

GoStrengths Inc. Fighting your bully with the power of humour. https://gostrengths.com/fighting-your-bully-with-the-power-of-humor/

Force, N. Throwing punch lines instead of punches. *PsychCentral* (online). https://psychcentral.com/blog/throwing-punch-lines-instead-of-punches/

Carter, J. (2019). How to have the last laughs when dealing with bullies. *American Management Association* (online). https://www.amanet.org/articles/how-to-have-the-last-laugh-when-dealing-with-lifes-bullies/

Face-Matching and Face-Recognition Software: the software that PC Maxine Carter used to compare photos of David Roberts and Marcus Beard exists and has been used extensively by police forces across the world. However, their use has been controversial:

Burgess, M. (2019). Inside the urgent battle to stop UK police using facial recognition. *Wired* (online), June 17th. https://www.wired.co.uk/article/uk-police-facial-recognition

Stokel-Walker, C. (2020). Is police use of face recognition now illegal in the UK? *New Scientist* (online), August 11th. https://www.newscientist.com/article/2251508-is-police-use-of-face-recognition-now-illegal-in-the-uk/

Picture Credits

De Courcy coat of arms:
https://en.wikipedia.org/wiki/John_de_Courcy

Ames Room Illusion photo
http://oceanswebsite.com/Amesroom1.html

Ames Room Illusion diagram
http://www.perceptionsense.com/2013/11/ames-room-explained.html

Read the First Paul Kanner Mystery
Clean-Out

Fourteen-year-old Paul Kanner spends his days playing chess, video-games, dreaming up scientific experiments and keeping his dog Bella amused...oh, and dodging his arch-nemesis John Cameron and his cronies.

While not-so-innocently whiling away his time in the neighbourhood streets, Paul becomes embroiled as a witness to one of a series of crimes that has baffled the Metropolitan Police for many years.

Through his association with the down-at-heel Sergeant Joe Bertolli and his friend Doctor Benjamin Zeigarnik, Paul is drawn into a mind-bending race to catch the mysterious criminal whom the police have dubbed 'Mr. Sheen'. Paul's life will never be the same again...

About the Author

Dr J D Demetre recently retired from his post of Principal Lecturer in Psychology at the University of Greenwich, London. He has held lectureships and research fellowships in Developmental Psychology at universities and institutes in the UK and the US.

He is a long-suffering supporter of Charlton Athletic Football Club and when not pulling his hair out at football matches can be found trying to converse with the family yorkiepoo or dodging the world from inside the covers of a book.